The House

that

Laughed

A novel by

Freda M. Chaney

Printed in the United States of America
First Edition
Black and White
March 7, 2017

∞

Book cover design by Freda M. Chaney
Book interior design by Freda M. Chaney

Front cover photo "Anne Hathaway Cottage"
by Freda M. Chaney, 2013

Back cover photo "Taking Time"
by Vicki L. Lowery, 2005

ISBN-13: 978-1542345156
ISBN-10: 1542345154

In loving memory of

Mildred Calista Chaney

1915-2017

∞

Member of

The Ladies Literary Society

Brazil, Indiana

Contents

Introduction

"To sleep,
perchance to dream
-ay, there's the rub."
- Shakespeare

What is life but a rich weaving of dreams: meandering thoughts from favorite books, a romantic fantasy that knits itself soul-deep, a favorite piece of art that captures the essence of you, poetry that plants itself in your literary garden, a hypnotic song that begs to be sung, a cozy house that draws you in and holds your heart forever.

Travel with twenty seven year old Miss Beck on her elusive journey into the unknown land of self. This straight-laced investigative journalist is all but a recluse who chooses her privacy and comfort over the social scene. Follow her as she takes a trip through literary illusion and back home to the real Sara Beck. Her life is pathetic, and she doesn't even know it. She is in a rut disguised as a life with no complications, until twenty nine year old Jacob Donnithorne steps in and turns her world upside down.

Join Sara on her exciting adventures through time as she explores the significance of friendship and love, ultimately forcing her to accept the unpredictability of life and relationships. This book will awaken your senses, and beg to be read again and again.

"It is never too late to be what

you might have been."

- Anon

Initiation

Dream

Chapter 1

"George, read to me."

"What shall I read, my dear?"

"Anything that speaks of somewhere but here."

"Settle back, Marian, and I will read until sleep finds you."

George Lewes began to read from Sir Walter Scott's poems as though his lover's life depended on it. "Just for you, my dear, from Scott's *Lady of the Lake*, Canto First, *The Chase*, verse XXV."

> The stranger viewed the shore around;
> Twas all so close with copsewood bound,
> Nor track nor pathway might declare
> That human foot frequented there,
> Until the mountain-maiden show'd
> A clambering, unsuspected road,
> That winded through the tangled screen,
> And open'd on a narrow green,
> Where weeping birch and willow round
> With their long fibres swept the ground.
> Here, for retreat in dangerous hour,
> Some chief had framed a rustic bower.

She slept soundly the rest of the night bathed in dreams of what might have been. George lifted his challenged body from the bed. How many nights had he sat at her side reassuring her? How many times had he read Scott to her, the cadence like her own voice, but at a lower octave? How much longer would this go on—her anxiety about publishing, and her deep regret about her family who wrecked her personality at a young age? He stumbled to the front parlor for some brandy. As he poured, he noticed her last manuscript stacked neatly on her pigeon-hole desk. He walked with his drink to examine her new manuscript with the working title, *Adam Bede*, a novel.

"You little frightened bird! little tearful rose! silly pet! You won't cry again, now I'm with you, will you?"

He mumbled to himself, "If publisher Blackwood sees this, he'll wonder if Marian's been taking too much Laudanum." He sat in her chair and scribbled notes with her dainty brass fountain pen, inserting mild suggestions into the text as he went. His comical sketches now and then would make her laugh. She depended on him. Always. Her fragile personality, her public image that made them travel each time one of her books was published. He set the pen back into Marian's inkwell stand. Moving along the dark hallway, he wondered what her next attack might be. It was never an overt attack. It was always something like a needy cry for help from deep inside the grown woman so many loved. Why could she not feel it—not see it—not understand that her past didn't matter, her ugliness didn't matter, her living with a married man did not matter to most who knew her well and loved her.

"I cannot save her. I must, however, show her how to save herself," he thought. George adjusted his pillow next to the novelist who had won England's hearts. The acrid smell of clove oil penetrated the Victorian bedroom. Marian was wrestling with a toothache again. George slept, but his sleep was never easy. Never. He was, after all, the companion of a high-strung, intellectual, "blue stocking" novelist whom he must protect from the world, from her family, from herself. The clock chimed twice in the hall outside the bedroom. George finally nodded off.

Victorian Trappings

Chapter 2

The maid brought breakfast to my door at 9:00 A.M. sharp. The dainty silver tray was laid with a simple white linen napkin and stainless steel ware. A heavy English breakfast of eggs sunny side up, bacon, broiled tomatoes, and buttered mushrooms flanked by strong black tea was placed strategically on the footed tray.

"Thank you, Mrs?"

"Miss. It's Miss." The waitress said in a soft tone. Will there be anything else, ma'am?"

"No thank you, Miss?"

"It's Miss Matthews."

"Miss Matthews it is then."

"Yes, ma'am."

"That sounds familiar."

"Will that be all, ma'am?"

"Yes, thank you." The waitress slipped out of the room and into the scarlet carpeted Victorian hallway.

The room was so authentic that it seemed I was in the Victorian period. I reached for the novel that lay at my side on the damask rose duvet cover. Inside the brown leather covers was an onion skin page protecting a simple print of George Eliot, the Victorian novelist. On the next page was an inscription to her husband. The book had drawn me in the night before. I read chapter one of *Adam Bede* and fell captive to its hypnotic wording. Eliot crafted her words like a master. She was like Houdini at the inkwell. And then, I remembered bits of a dream from the night before. It seemed real!

Sitting upright in the antique mahogany bed, I minced at my breakfast. No doubt it was prepared by a cook working at minimum wage in the front kitchen. I had never eaten a breakfast that big. From all appearances, I might have been in England just that moment, settled into a manor house sipping tea and buttering scones. It felt that way—as if I were there. I looked around to be sure my traveling cases were still near the door. Yes. And my shoes were tucked neatly under the edge of the bed.

I thumbed through the old novel with one hand while picking at my breakfast with the other. Meanwhile, somewhere on a page of *Adam Bede*, young Hetty Sorrel prepared for a long day of butter-making in the dairy.

There was a knock at the door. "Who is it?"

"Your room maid, Miss Matthews."

"Come in. The door is unlocked."

The white cap on Miss Matthews' head was askew as she peeked around the door. "How is your breakfast?"

"It is a bit much, Miss Matthews!"

"Oh? May I get you something else, ma'am?"

"As a matter of fact, I would like to know about the history of this house. It feels so authentic here!"

"There is a scrapbook full of information in the front entry. Have you filled out your guest card yet, ma'am?"

"Guest card?"

"Yes, ma'am. It is a guest wish list that is to be returned to the front desk. You requested the Eliot Room, so we thought you might like the Victorian period package? You will find your courtesy card on your desk."

"What comes with the Victorian package, Miss Matthews?"

"That is up to you, ma'am."

"Odd!"

"What is that, ma'am?"

"Oh nothing, I was just saying how interesting it is here—almost like I stepped into another time and place."

"They all say that, ma'am. Most guests just need to get away. Rosehill is the ultimate getaway."

"Yes, it is. I've been pressed at work. Experience?"

"Just fill out the card, ma'am, and the rest is self-explanatory."

"I'll do that, Miss Matthews." Her mushroom-capped head disappeared, and the door closed with a heavy thud.

"What on Earth was that?" I was beginning to talk to myself. I reached for my phone sitting on a tea-stained lace doily on the nightstand. I dialed Mr. Cooper's direct number at *The Times Herald*.

"Enjoying your stay?" He cleared his throat waiting for my response.

"What is this place? You said it was a relaxing get-away, not a museum of experiences!"

"Now Beck, don't put up your guard against having a new experience. Relax. Enjoy. Go with the flow!" The sound of the squeaky spring and the raspy spark of the lighter told me Mr. Cooper was tipped back in his office chair lighting the stub of a leftover cigar.

"Are you smoking again? Listen, I need to find out more about this place. How did you book my stay, and what is the record of activity here for say the last five years?"

"Will you calm down!" I could hear him adjusting nervously in his cheap vinyl chair.

"Hello? Are you still there, Mr. Cooper?"

"Yes, yes! Damn, give me some time to inhale! The staff and I thought it might be a nice place for you to go while getting over that numbskull who broke your heart. The loser!"

I heard the raspy lighter again as Mr. Cooper relit his cigar stub. There was a brief silence as he drew in a deep breath. "Quit being the overly inquisitive journalist, and relax for a change." Mr. Cooper's voice trailed off into the background as he dismissed his stenographer from her duties in front of his desk.

"Is someone there with you? Why didn't you tell me? You have me on speaker phone, don't you? Oh my god, I can't keep anything private anymore!"

"In the world of news, nothing is private, Beck! You know that."

"I'm hanging up now! See what you can find and call me back."

"Who's the boss?" Mr. Cooper dropped the phone onto its cradle with a bang. I felt violated—by my boss, by the office staff, by my ex-boyfriend. Perhaps Mr. Cooper was right; I need to get away from it all. Oh, if only I could live in a simpler time.

I reached again for the antiquated copy of *Adam Bede* by George Eliot. The book opened at chapter 2. Feeling lucky, I began to read.

> About a quarter of seven there was an unusual appearance of excitement in the village of Hayslope, and through the whole length of its little street, from the Donnithorne Arms to the church-yard gate, the inhabitants had evidently been drawn out of their houses by something more than the pleasure of lounging in the evening sunshine.

Suddenly something was shoved under the door. I rose from the overstuffed bed to see what it was. Surely Mr. Cooper paid the bill! I struggled to remember how long I was scheduled to be there. I lifted the folded paper and read,

"Welcome, Miss Beck. We are delighted to have you with us for your Victorian experience. Please fill out the guest card so that we can better serve your needs. You are scheduled for one week, but should you change your mind and want to stay longer, please do advise us before your initial week expires. Please respect the privacy of other guests in the historical period rooms so that their experiences are not disrupted. You may not share your experience with another guest, and they may not share with you. Sincerely, Miss Brook, Manager"

What *is* this place? I should check out now. At that moment, I felt vulnerable, like I was free falling with no possibility of nets.

I missed my friend, my companion. But I could not call, not now. He was with another. I felt like a princess who'd lost her castle and prince. I'd had it all. What's left, but this weird experience of feeling out of sync with my surroundings. Was this a mental institution? A haunted house?

I stood upright and looked around the room. The only modern items in that overdone Victorian boudoir were my things that I brought in my traveling cases. They prove that I'm sane! I ran to my cases, and unzipped them. My large case was packed with vintage fashions. My eyes could not believe what they saw! On top was a crimson velvet gown with rhinestone buttons. Brussels' lace spilled over the thick skirt like a waterfall.

My own things were nowhere to be found. Wait! There was my smart phone, my keepsake watch, and my simple sterling silver earrings at the bedside. I scooped them up like winnings at a card table. These are my link to sanity, I thought. I stuffed them into my robe pockets. I must have put on the robe the night before. It was floor length creamy silk with initials on the right lapel. G. E. Who was G.E.?

I rang the bell for service, but no one came. They must have been on break. I needed my own clothes! I rummaged through the wardrobe and found a simple long skirt and a lace blouse that fit my slight figure perfectly. I looked like a fuddy-duddy, but it would have to do. There was no one to carry luggage, so I grabbed my leather cases, stepped out of the suite and into the hall. I escaped through the front door of the strange B & B.

Rerouting Time

Chapter 3

The wild honeysuckle tickled my nose as I bent to breathe in the scent deeply. It was refreshing to leave the stuffy Victorian B & B. Although its exterior was an authentic, brightly painted lady, the interior was dark and brooding. Mr. Cooper would be ticked about my checking out early. He had paid for the stay assuming I needed something as different from my stark neutral surroundings as he could find. Rosehill B & B was the only one for miles around. They weren't so popular here. We liked our concierge hotels and access to high speed internet. And where were the roses at Rosehill? I looked around quickly before grasping the leather handles on my traveling cases. Not a single rose.

"Ma'am," shouted a voice from the front steps, "you forgot this." The room maid handed me a certificate for the balance of my stay. "Now don't forget to fill out your guest card should you decide to return."

"Of course." I turned from the maid, dismissing her, Rosehill, and the room that nearly absorbed me with its velvet, lace, and silk. It was rude of me, but I was used to being rude. I'd spent my adult years as a journalist— more of a sleuth really. In every coat and jacket I owned was a lined tablet and simple pen, just in case. My cat would be glad to see me, but it wouldn't fuss over me as a dog might. I hated fussing.

Through the over-arching branches of the apple trees, the early morning sunlight peeped. I decided to go directly back to my apartment. I'd sit with the cat I'd never named, that's how Holly Golightly did it in *Breakfast at Tiffany's*. My whole life was trim, spare, minimal. I didn't like intrusions, and the office staff at work knew not to come to my door without scheduling days in advance.

Cat was glad to see me, but kept his tail swipes at three. We understood each other. I snapped on the lights in the hallway. It was an older apartment building, refinished in the 1990s to modernize its turn-of-the-century look. Its ceilings were tall with suspended fans in most rooms. The windows climbed up the ten foot walls to meet the transom. I had a habit of leaving the top windows ajar to allow fresh air in. Turning the corner from the hall, I heard movement in the living room! I reached for my emergency mace. Cat didn't seem agitated, so it must be a breeze coming through the transom windows.

"Miss Beck?" It was my neighbor who was watching Cat for me while I was away.

"Jenny?"

"You're home early. So sorry." She jumped up from the sofa like a soldier at attention.

"Where is he?"

"In the bathroom, Miss Beck. Please don't be harsh with him. This was my idea—a chance to be alone."

"Just clear out when you can, but first get him out of my bathroom! Here is the money I owe you for sitting Cat." I threw two twenty dollar bills on the table to cover the wages for one day. Jenny and her boyfriend walked like tiptoeing mice down the hall, latching the door behind them.

Home. This was my place of belonging to something. It was like walking into a fresh bowl of Grandmother's macaroni and cheese. The faint smell of wine entered my world. The little sneak had found my wine stash! I found the half-drunk bottle and dumped the dregs down the drain. Opening a new Chardonnay by Dutcher Crossing of California, I dropped into the overstuffed sectional and tipped the glass. Cat watched, then napped.

The wine, the neutral colors around the room, Michael Buble piping from my stereo, brought me back to myself. Simple, easy, nothing fussy. Just comfy. Photos of loved ones flanked the living room on low tables and high shelves. They were mostly black and white with an occasional sepia tone.

Ugh! I just remembered that scoundrel who dumped me for the blonde with blue eyes. He said he loved brunettes with brown eyes. She had everything it would seem, including him, but I still had my self-respect. I did not require people or things to complete me. Men like independent women.

My phone chimed. Was it my ex? No, he's with her. He didn't miss me. I'm too plain—too intellectual.

"Miss Beck here."

"Beck, it's Mr. Cooper!"

"Yes, Mr. Cooper, I know your voice after working at the paper for five years!"

"Listen, Beck, I have an assignment for you."

"I don't think so! You shuffled me off to that B & B from hell, and thought I'd write about the experience there. For what?"

"You are as stubborn as any mule I've known!" Mr. Cooper yelled through the phone.

"Oh, and how many mules have you known in your life, Mr. Cooper?"

"Oh, for god sake, Beck. I was just trying to help."

"Help, like my father might help?"

"Look, I'm sorry he wasn't there for you, and I'm sorry your boyfriend went for a blonde, but you need to keep busy doing what you do best. Work helps!"

"You don't have to tell me that. I am committed to my work at *The Times Herald.*"

"Prove it!" Mr. Cooper challenged.

"Why you infuriating piece of..," I stumbled for the perfect word. "Work! Piece of work—that's what you are, Mr. Cooper!"

But Mr. Cooper had long since hung up the phone. By now he was tipped back in his chair smiling, the stub of a cigar sandwiched between his teeth. I beat the throw cushion on the back of the sofa. Mr. Cooper was right, though I'd never admit it! Ever! My father had ruled the roost, and my boyfriend tried to rule me. I'd have none of it!

Second Street Diner

Chapter 4

I slept on the sofa all night. It was comforting backed up against the support of the overstuffed cushions. I surveyed the room before rising to make sure there were no remnants of Rosehill around. I showered and dressed in simple straight slacks with a matching khaki blouse. I had to meet Mr. Cooper, that obnoxious old grump! The staff thought him gruff and old-fashioned, but my reaction was more overt. Something about him unnerved me! He was a temperamental editor like the Mr. Grant character in the *Mary Tyler Moore Show* reruns. Though I didn't want to hear what Mr. Cooper had to say, I wanted to know more about his assignment. I'd traveled a bit writing for his paper. Where to now?

Outside a misty rain punctuated the boxwood hedges with pearly liquid mirrors. Today was another day of typical spring weather for the Upper Midwest. It was a playground of mud puddles for kids who grew up here. The only thing better was sledding in winter. I popped up my umbrella and walked with a decided step to my car, a beige Buick LaSabre, purchased when I was nineteen. It got me to my first job after high school, and through college. I shook my umbrella, threw it on the back passenger floor, and started the car. It was all so simple—this way of life. No one to tell me what to do, when to do it, or even if I should or should not do it. This was my world full of me, no one else but.

I reflected for a moment. I'd lost my father and mother to my need for independence. My twin sisters resented me because I was living the life they would live if they could. I envied them for their commitment to raising a family, but they did not see it honorable themselves. Their husbands liked having them at home, but respected working women who held professional positions. It was all over them at office parties. My sisters called to complain at least once a year. Other than that, I didn't hear from them. They never came to Worthing as lovely as it was with its parks, a historical theater, cafes that served up tall lattes that matched any Starbucks served. They didn't grow up here, and so it was not their place to call home. Staying was easier, especially for twins. They resisted the city with its contract for cleverness. I left my hometown in rural Ohio to struggle my way through small local papers to one with a national reputation. *The Times Herald* was no *New York Times*, but it kept me busy and away from milking cows like some of my childhood friends were doing.

The drive into the inner city was challenging because of the work traffic and inclement weather. I switched on satellite radio. The Bee Gees blended with mist outside my car singing "Nobody gets too much heaven no more. It's harder to come by. I'm waiting in line...." Isn't that the truth! My phone chimed, bringing me back to my safe space surrounded by leather. I let Blue tooth technology do its wonders. "Miss Beck here! With whom am I speaking?" It could be a publisher, or a response to that application I submitted to *Just Facts* magazine, so I put on my Miss Beck hat and spoke like a secretary. I found it all so amusing.

"Beck?"

"I'm on my way, Mr. Cooper!"

"Listen, I've been thinking." I laughed aloud at his ridiculous statement. It was one of his favorite things to say. Of course he was thinking! "Will you meet me at the diner on Second Street in half an hour?"

"That cheesy diner? Oh, Mr. Cooper! Do I have to?"

"I'll pay." His voice trailed off. No amount of money would make it worth my while to sit in one of those red vinyl booth seats that sink down to the floor. I always felt like a kindergartner on a school bus. And Mr. Cooper would order up a huge plate of something covered in gravy. Save me! The smell alone was enough to start me retching. I dialed Mr. Cooper back. His voice mail took my message.

"Damn! Nothing to do but drive to the diner now. He never answers his cellphone. I don't blame him; it was a step above a Jitterbug with huge buttons. The worn numbers almost required Braille. It folded in half like the 1970s Star Trek communicator. The entire office staff would wait for it—the moment Mr. Cooper yanked his antiquated phone from his oversized pockets and flipped it open like he was Captain Kirk summoning Mr. Spock to the bridge.

I swung my car into a parking lot behind the diner. There I wouldn't have to worry about dents and scratches even if I had to walk farther. The morning mist had lifted. A shaft of sunlight played on my face. I grabbed my umbrella and leather briefcase from the back, and headed to the diner door. There it was, the Second Street Diner in all of its glory with a half-hinged neon sign with two letters burned out! Lovely. I could see Mr. Cooper through the fogged front window sitting at his favorite seat. He loved news, and was always sniffing for a story.

"Beck! Over here!" Mr. Cooper yelled.

"Yes." How could I not know where he was in that small diner with eight booths and a half dozen tables at its center? I blushed, looking around to see if anyone heard Mr. Cooper yell.

"Mr. Cooper, how are you today, Sir?" He was already eating his biscuits and gravy and tossing back a black liquid that resembled coffee.

"Sit, Beck." He continued to mop his plate of gravy with another oversized biscuit.

"What is on your mind, Mr. Cooper?"

"Order up! Then we'll talk."

"I'm not very hungry."

"At least get a donut and coffee. You're too thin!"

"The coffee is repulsive and the donuts are so large that no self-respecting female would eat one in a sitting. I guess I'll have some Melba toast and a cup of tea with honey."

"You order that. I won't embarrass myself." Mr. Cooper was not kidding. I called the waitress and put in my order. She laughed on her way back to the kitchen.

"Well, what did you want to see me about, Mr. Cooper?"

He licked gravy from his lips, and spoke up, directing his gaze at me as though I were under a spotlight in a police station. "Beck, you owe me the money back for the six days that you did not stay at the Rosehill B & B."

"What?"

"Don't look so shocked. We had a deal that you would take some time off. Now, either you pay me for six days lodging, or you do something else for me."

"What!"

"Stop saying WHAT! You look like a possum in headlights. Here comes your order. Eat up, and I will do the talking. I need someone to travel to England for me to check out some timeshare properties. I think you are the perfect candidate to fly over the pond and take a look see. Maybe you could learn to eat breakfast there too!"

"I have eaten British breakfast, Mr. Cooper."

I reached for my briefcase. "I will pay you with this certificate for six remaining days. Here!" I shoved the Rosehill gift certificate at him indignantly.

"Seriously? You want me to stay at the Rosehill B & B? I would be the laughing stock!" He lifted his chin indignantly.

"You booked it for me, so you must have thought it was the cat's meow!"

"No, I booked it for you because I thought you needed time away, and the office staff thought it was something a lady would enjoy."

"I see." I dived back into my briefcase, spilling the contents. "Here's my contract with you, Mr. Cooper. It says nothing about staying at the Rosehill as part of my job description."

"What's that? Do you always carry your job contract in your briefcase? And vintage novels?"

"Vintage what?" I looked down at the items I had spilled from my briefcase onto the sunken red vinyl seat beside me. "*Adam Bede!* This is the novel I was reading at Rosehill. I must return it!"

"I'll return it, and have a look around the place," Mr. Cooper insisted. "Meanwhile, I want you to fly to England! No changing my mind. Here is your ticket. Your plane leaves in a week."

Mr. Cooper went back to eating his breakfast while I sipped tea and turned my attention back to *Adam Bede*, if only to avoid watching my infuriating boss slurp his gravy. I immersed myself in chapter two, "The Preaching" of George Eliot's first novel.

The Donnithorne Arms stood at the entrance of the village, and a small farm-yard and stack-yard which flanked it, indicating that there was a pretty take of land attached to the inn, gave the traveler a promise of good feed for himself and his horse, which might well console him for the ignorance in which the weather-beaten sign left him as to the heraldic bearings of that ancient family, the Donnithornes.

Who were the Donnithornes, and how did they fit into the plot of Eliot's novel? Did she know a prominent British family for whom she'd named the characters? I suddenly felt like doing some detective work. "Mr. Cooper, I am going to take this book back to Rosehill myself."

"Do as you like, Beck, but be on that plane next week!"

I darted from the Second Street Diner with a new direction—a new story—possibly the plot for my own first novel.

Returning to Rosehill

Chapter 5

The evening sun was laying patches on the Worthing fields highlighting the spindly wheat-colored poverty grass and ghastly mounds of multiflora rose. There were no sheep in the fields because the farmers had driven them, with the help of a faithful shepherding dog, down to the pen for the night. Therein was safety. The scene reminded me of the countryside of Thomas Hardy's novel *Far from the Madding Crowd.*

Finally Rosehill B & B came into view. The winding road gave the pink lady an air of mystique, though it hardly needed the snaking drive to make it look more mysterious. I put on the parking brake, and made my way to the massive front door. I pulled the ceramic knob doorbell. The deep sound of chimes seeped through the sidelight windows. The door opened slowly.

"Good evening, ma'am. Did you bring your guest card with you?" The maid smiled sweetly.

"No, I'm only here to return this book to you before someone else reserves the Eliot Room. I only meant to borrow it. I feel so ashamed to have packed it away in my briefcase. I guess I was in a hurry to check out, and wasn't paying attention to what I was doing."

"Oh no, ma'am. The book is yours to keep. It is part of the package. You will find many more such books in your room: *Romola, Daniel Deronda, Theophrastus Such....*"

"*Theophrastus Such*? What kind of book title is that?"

"It's George Eliot, ma'am. Just follow me." The maid motioned me toward the mahogany door at the end of the long front hall.

"Not tonight, but I will return for the other books later." I was sure I looked nervous as I began to back away.

"Later, ma-am?"

"I won't be staying tonight. Cat needs me. And I must prepare for a trip to England."

"Indeed you must prepare, and pack plenty of heavy clothes for your trip; tonight there is to be a mighty storm! Farmer Newburne already brought his sheep to the bank barn just beyond the hill. That means trouble's brewing." She motioned again toward the Victorian door at the end of the hall. "I'll make you some strong tea if you like."

"You don't understand. I'm not staying. I don't have clothes to wear, and Cat is alone at my apartment."

There was a sudden crashing sound. I jumped. Was I hit? "The storm has started, ma'am!" The maid helped me over the threshold. I did not resist.

"You will find all you need behind the door. I'll be there promptly with your tea." Tea did sound good just then, so I followed the maid down the dim hallway, the George Eliot novel tucked under my arm. I repeatedly said *"Theophrastus Such"* as I went, wondering who on earth would title a book in such a way. However, I did like the full round sound of the book she titled *Middlemarch*. I had been, after all, marching in the middle of things most of my life—never committing to one thing or another except my job. I needed a pushpin in the bulletin board of my life to hold me to the one gift I could keep and give away at the same time—the words I wrote daily for *The Times Herald*.

"There you go!" She eased the door open to reveal a slightly different setting than the one I'd seen earlier in the Eliot Room. "Do not worry. You'll be perfectly comfortable, ma'am. It will feel like your home away from home." There was a meow as the ten-foot door swung closed behind her. Was there was a parlor cat?

I set my things on the bed and checked around the room to see if there were remnants of my previous stay. The décor was different as though a significant amount of time had passed.

Inside the wardrobe, the clothing styles were mostly free of lace, and not a scarlet frock among them. I breathed a sigh of relief. Oddly, though, there were men's and women's clothing. The men's cutaway jackets seemed small even for Victorian wear. A beaver top hat sat high on the top shelf like it owned the wardrobe.

A small green granite box sat beside it, almost daring me to open it. I did. There were diamond cufflinks, a gold pocket watch and fob. A photo of someone quite beautiful lay under the jewelry. The female was captive in black velvet and had golden brown hair and stunning blue-gray eyes. Her cheeks were roses. Who is this lovely lady, and how is she associated with the gentleman who owned the top hat and jewelry?

I pulled one of the embroidered nightgowns and a dressing robe from the wardrobe. There were initials, but they were too ornate to make them out. Around the letters was a ring of stitched rosebuds. The gown and robe were obviously not mass produced in a factory. It was the finest hand stitching I'd ever seen.

A pair of delicate ivory boots rested on the floor next to the bed. They looked much too small for me. I snuggled into the big bed which had donned a fresh mauve duvet cover. While I waited for the maid to bring tea, I read more of Eliot's novel, *Adam Bede*. It was not the book I would choose to read if it were not part of this "experience." The introductory chapters were rather solemn and religious-sounding. That was not me. That was not my way of life.

My feet felt cold, so out of desperation I tried the ivory boots. They seemed long and thin, not at all like the shape of my own foot, but buttery soft—like calfskin.

There was a knock at the door. "Come in!"

"Here's your tea, ma'am." The maid set the small silver tray on a marble stand between two pink reading chairs on either side of the fireplace. "Will there be anything else?"

"Yes, can you tell me about these boots and clothes? How did you change the décor so quickly? And that meowing? Is there a cat in this house? Do you have rodents?"

"Change the décor, ma'am? I don't believe we have. Perhaps you have done so?" She studied me for some sign of agreement. "As for the clothing, you will find all you need at your disposal. Feel free to wear it into the common rooms, but please don't enter the other guests' rooms. You may meet them in the dining room each evening at 6:00 P.M. for supper. The boots belonged to someone somewhere is all I can tell you. It appears they fit you perfectly and will serve you well. Cat? We have no cat. No rodents either, ma'am."

I was stunned. I knew the maid was watching me intently for signs of instability. And at that moment I felt unstable, lost, searching for something I was yet unfamiliar with—a wild experience, *un air d' escapade*. The maid turned away after a diminutive curtsy and closed the huge wall of a door behind her. It was just me and this room now—me and these clothes—me and the pair of shifty boots that became my size when I put them on. It was me and this leather-bound book titled *Adam Bede*. I wondered if there were bugs in old books as I flipped through frantically searching for anything that moved.

I dropped into one of the plush high back reading chairs and poured a cup of tea. The rich aroma of the British blend poured from the spout. I heard the tea ball rattle inside the pot. Replacing the teapot cozy, I lifted the dainty white porcelain cup to drink. As I did, something caught my eye in the corner. There was movement! "Mice!" I screamed. I waited for further evidence, mortified in every possible way. Then, three taps on the flooring as though a hand were moving beneath the fabric. "Oh my god!" I jumped up into the the reading chair, spilling my tea as I went. My eyes were bulging with disbelief as I waited for the big reveal. Out from under the edge of the skirted fainting couch crawled Cat!

My heart was pounding like that of the murderer in Edgar Allen Poe's short story *The Telltale Heart!* "Cat, you nearly gave me a heart attack!" Cat sauntered over to me, striking my leg three times with his tail, then off he went to explore. Cat was not used to seeing me alarmed, and chose to walk away rather than to be attentive to my needs. I had always liked Cat because he didn't need me. I didn't need Cat either, or at least I thought so until now. It was good to see him waltzing around the room investigating the floor, the furniture, the bookcases. But how on earth did he get here? Mr. Cooper? Maybe he thought I needed my pet for support. Feeling safer somehow with Cat in my presence, I poured more tea and finished it as I read hungrily a few more passages of *Adam Bede*. Eliot was an amazing word weaver. I would give anything to know how to write as well as this author, or Austen, or Bronte.

The walnut grandfather clock in the hall sounded eleven chimes. The deep tones were like old church bells that never lose their true ring. I set the novel on the tea stand, and walked around the room to find Cat. No sign of him. I was not about to crawl under the bed or fainting couch. He could be anywhere. I pulled down the mountainous duvet cover and slipped into bed. The starched linens scratched my skin. I smelled lavender near the headboard, and looked to see the fragrant bundled stems on each post. It was soothing, and soon, I drifted off to sleep.

What Doesn't Kill Us
Dream

Chapter 6

"Where is my hot water bottle, George? I believe I left it here at my footstool when I was reading Wordsworth to you this afternoon. I do not see it anywhere." The embroidered footstool sitting near the fender at the fireplace invited Marian once again. She sat in the high back chair propping her feet in her usual manner, and retrieving a book from the side table. It was the book from which George had so lovingly read to her many nights before, Scott's *Lady of the Lake*. "Where did you last stop reading, George?"

"What's that, Marian?" George murmured from the next room. He parted the gathered, gaudy curtains at the water closet entrance, and stepped into the sitting room where his companion was holding one of her most precious volumes.

"Ah, yes, *Lady of the Lake*, Canto First, verse XXV. I read to the end of the verse. Before I started the next, you were fast asleep. How is your toothache, dearest? Here is your hot water bottle. I took it into the kitchen and had Beatrice boil fresh water and fill it." Marian reached for the familiar water bottle and placed it under her ivory-slippered feet.

"So, no toothache today?"

"None. I will read another verse or two from Canto First, and then I will get back to my writing." She spoke nothing more as she ran her long thin fingers across the lines of the book pages. She was immersed into the world of Sir Walter Scott, her hero since childhood.

George went on talking as though Marian was hanging onto his every word. He was an animated little man with a starched white collar, a black cutaway coat, a black cravat, black shoes, and dark hair that seemed to fall in strings about his head. "Marian, I'm going out to meet Spencer today. He has this manuscript he wants me to look over. He's not been well you know. Herbert is a high-strung nervous sort. He's been rattling on about evolution. He is paranoid that someone will steal his ideas. I must do something to help him, if only to stroll with him in London. For some reason, he likes to feed the pigeons along the Thames. Ahh, there's where I'd love to live one day. How about you, Marian? Marian?" His mate was not ignoring him; she was engrossed in Scott at that moment. She read aloud as he placed his beaver hat atop his curls and kissed her cheek.

> It was a lodge of ample size,
> But strange of structure and device;
> Of such materials, as around the workman's
> Hand had readiest found;
> Lopp'd off their boughs,
> Their hoar trunks bared,
> And by the hatchet rudely squared.
> To give their walls the destined height
> The sturdy oak and ash unite;
> While moss and clay and leaves combin'd

To fence each crevice from the wind,
The lighter pine trees over-head,
Their slender length for rafters spread,
And wither'd heath and rushes dry
Supplied a russet canopy.

"That's exquisite, Marian. Now I'm off!"

"Off—to where—to see whom?"

"Dear Marian, I am off to see Spencer. I am concerned about his changeable moods. I will walk with him along the Thames, smoke a cigar, feed the pigeons, and maybe stop for some sweets for you on the way home."

"Oh, George, you know I can't have treats with this bad tooth."

"We must get you in to see the tooth doctor."

"When I'm finished writing the first installment of my new novel, *Sister Maggie*—then I can care for myself without a fit of conscience for neglecting my work."

"Suit yourself, Marian." He pulled his ornate walking stick from the umbrella stand and marched to the front door. Marian watched his every step. She adored the little man whom no one else understood. She would watch the door until he came home. Such was her insecurity. *What if he went back to Agnes?* While George Lewes was away, she would dream, reimagine, and write about places of her childhood from a sudden nostalgic memory, molding the people from her native Warwickshire into characters for her first novel. In her mind, she would walk again the grounds of Griff to show all who read her work how much she loved, and missed her homestead since Isaac had taken over its care. Isaac—her brother and boyhood playmate, now reduced to a pathetic, judgmental miser counting out the family's money and dispensing it as he saw fit. Marian was left to depend on her writing, both for herself and for George Lewes, the married man for whom she'd given up everything. "What doesn't kill us, makes for great writing." she wrote in a journal on that day in 1859.

The sun went down, and still no George. Marian fretted and went to bed, weeping under the covers for the man she loved.

Sniffing Out a Story

Chapter 7

Cat was still in hiding. No sign of movement in the room. No smell. No sound except those made by the clinking of dishes as the breakfast trays were set on hall stands. I lay back on the mahogany headboard and waited for the knock on my door. I occupied the last room at the end of the hall. It was a prominent room that could be easily seen from the Rosehill front door. I wondered what the other rooms looked like.

"Ma'am? Your breakfast," came the voice at my door.

"Door is open!"

"Good morning! Did you sleep well?"

"After a bit of excitement!"

"Excitement, ma'am?"

"My cat somehow sneaked into my room last night. I was frightened beyond belief! It was hiding under the fainting couch over there. Scared me nearly to death. I spilled tea on the reading chair—the one on the right. Sorry."

"Cat? What did it look like?"

"Well, it was a Tabby, gray with beautiful green eyes. I think it was my cat that I call Cat. But I sure don't understand how he got here!"

"Oh, no, ma'am. That was not your cat. There are no live cats here."

"No live cats? What do you mean by that?"

"Well, I mean it was probably the ghost of a stray cat that was allowed to wander inside this home a century or more ago. The story is that somehow it got trapped in the house after it was abandoned. No one knew it was here. When the new owners opened the house up after all of those years, there was the carcass of the cat on the kitchen floor. It must have been waiting for its meal."

"That's terrible! So why would the cat be in this room if it died in the kitchen?"

"It wandered the house freely, but this was its favorite room, ma'am."

"Perfect! What was its name?"

"It had no name. They called it by its breed, Tabby. It was just a mouser for the property as the story goes. But the old lady who lived here in the 1800s was afraid of mice, so allowed Tabby to keep her company at night in her room—this room. Well, so the story goes."

"What next?"

"Ma'am?"

"Nothing, I'm just wondering what insane thing will happen to me next. The dreams, the décor, the clothes, the boots, the cat!"

"You will feel better after breakfast." The maid was the size of a minute, but wielded a silver tray like no one I'd seen before. She set the tray on my bed, angling it just so for my convenience. "Would you like me to pour your tea?"

"No thank you, but I would like a morning paper, *The Times Herald*, please."

"We don't receive the paper here, ma'am. I can bring you some periodicals."

"No newspapers? No television? No radio?"

"No, ma'am."

"Never mind. I'll dress after breakfast and go out to find a newspaper."

The maid stepped to the door, turned and smiled. It was one of those smiles that make you feel uneasy—like there is no reason to be smiling just now!

The tea was more comforting than usual, but why? Just then I remembered a movie I'd watched about a lady named Lily. Her friends turned against her, and she became an outcast of society. Near the end of the movie, she has a comforting cup of tea. Was her name

Lily Bart? That sounds right. What is the name of that movie? *House of Mirth*? Yes, it was inspired by Edith Wharton's book by the same title. Lily's mother had passed away, and her dowager aunt took her in and introduced her to society. Lily took too many risks, and the aunt disapproved. She left her fortune to another relative, and Lily had to work for a living.

In the end Lily is renting a room, eating little, and drugging herself to sleep. She commits suicide rather than expose the friend who betrayed her. The final scene brings her one true love to her bedside as he weeps and tells the still body on the bed that he loves her. In life, she would not allow herself to rely on men for support. Men proposed to her, but she refused. Lily was full of pride, but she was a good friend to the end.

Wow, all that from a cup of tea! I needed to get out of the room! I was not just asking myself questions, I was answering them too!

I was determined to investigate the rest of the house—well as far as I could get before they caught me and reminded me of the restrictions! The common areas would be the safe place to start. Maybe I could find that scrapbook Miss Matthews mentioned my first day here.

I finished my tea and toast, and left the rest of the British style breakfast on the tray. I decided to try the copper tub. It was surrounded by a semi-circular ring of white curtains trimmed with a gold crown motif. I ran a bath and climbed in, propping a towel under my neck for comfort. I could get used to this, I thought.

My mind drifted to the dream I'd had the night before. Why was I having these dreams—here in this room—dreams I'd never had before. I struggled to remember the details, but they were so vague. Some lady was weeping under a blanket. Yes. Her man had broken her heart. Or did he? I remember now—he was late coming home. She needed him to be there for her. She was a nervous type—fretful, and yet she was strong inwardly with a heart of gold. Who was that greasy little man who left her alone and spent the day in London? Who did he think he was stepping out on her in his cutaway coat and top hat? I hurt for the woman in the dream—so much like my own life.

After a long soak, I dressed in an olive print floor length skirt and a white blouse with minimal lace around the neck and cuffs. I wore the ivory boots for want of a pair of flats in the wardrobe. I might kill myself in those tie up, heeled boots! My hair lay loose on my neck as I entered the hallway through the massive door.

"Miss Beck?"

"Yes, Miss Brook? How are you?"

"I'm so pleased you have returned to complete your experience."

"I had no choice. There was a storm brewing last night, and I couldn't risk turning back for home after I came to return your book."

"Storm? What storm, Miss Beck?"

"The maid said that there was a huge storm coming in, and that farmer Newburne put his sheep in the pen early for protection."

"The maid is daffy, Miss Beck. Pay no mind to her. Did you hear a storm?"

"No, but I was much involved with the cat in my room."

"Cat? We allow no pets."

"Oh? More of the daffy maid stories then? But wait— I saw the cat with my own eyes!"

"This old house plays tricks, Miss Beck. It is best to let things go as soon as you experience them. Life teaches us lessons at any moment. Always look for the good in the lesson, and let it go."

"I see." So we are back to the experience of the place.

"Allow me to take you to the salon, Miss Beck."

"I always wear my hair this way. It's simple—easy— no fuss."

"Indeed, it is all that, but here at Rosehill, you'll want something a bit more proper, Miss Beck. Follow me." My heart was pounding. Miss Brook led the way down the hall, refusing any suggestions I made to the contrary. She opened double doors into a spectacular room full of button-tufted chairs with matching stools.

There were seven vanity mirrors against the walls. In the center of the room, a large round table topped with white linen was home to a huge urn filled with multi-colored, cut flowers.

"Where is everyone?"

"Everyone?"

"Yes? The other guests?"

"They are in their rooms finishing breakfast, Miss Beck. They will be along shortly. You ate little of your breakfast this morning. I hope you will eat more from now on. Was everything to your liking?"

"I'm not a big eater—never have been. I like tea and toast for breakfast."

"We'll remember that, Miss Beck, and hope that your appetite improves with your experience here. Please be seated and someone will be along to coif your hair."

"Coif my hair?" Miss Brook walked away, turning to face me, then closing the doors with both hands as she stepped backwards. After what seemed about five minutes, the doors opened again. In stepped a beautiful woman wearing a floor length black dress and a long white apron. I assumed she was the hairdresser.

"Good morning, Miss." She smiled like the room maid. "If you will turn yourself toward the vanity, I will pin your hair for you."

"Pin my hair? I would just like it brushed."

"Oh no, Miss, here we do one style for ladies, and one style for men. I can add combs if you like, or maybe a sprig of fresh flowers?"

"Combs would be fine." My voice sounded rude, but wasn't rudeness part of my personality? "Mr. Cooper is going to hear it from me!"

"What's that, ma'am?"

"Oh, nothing!" I sat back in the button-tufted chair, finding it quite comfortable. It felt good having someone brush my hair. My mother had been too busy with my younger twin sisters to brush and style my hair. I was always brushing theirs. I succumbed to the comfort of it all, closed my eyes and napped.

"Will that be all, ma'am?"

"Oh.., yes!" I awoke with a start, realizing the lady had piled my hair on top of my head securing it with two ornate combs. I scarcely recognized myself. The mirror was lying.

"I'll excuse myself then, and you may like to join the other guests in the sitting room."

"Thank you for the lovely hairstyle. I've never worn my hair up like this. I've seen pictures of the 1960s hairdos—the beehive—looked a bit silly. But this style looks elegant.

I bid her a good day, and looked at myself in the mirror just long enough to smile a time or too. Out of the double doors I went sniffing for clues to the best story I may ever write for Mr. Cooper. Or *was* it for Mr. Cooper? Maybe this story was just for me.

Common Ground

Chapter 8

The windowed door to the sitting room was open just a crack. The lace curtains hugged the beveled glass and draped to the floor. The scene was one of gentility, of high society—a bygone time. As I stood peeping in through the slightly open door, I surmised that although this was a Victorian parlor, not all of the guests were dressed in Victorian clothing.

"Entre vous," came a voice as sweet as white petaled flowers.

"Merci," I said to the French maid just inside the door. She fluffed the skirt of my gown as I passed. For a petite figure, she was commanding in her black and white uniform trimmed in lace. She stretched her arm and pointed toward a table where seven guests were gathered around a bowl of punch. I walked slowly to join them.

"Do you have a partner?" came the deep voice of a man standing close to the punch bowl.

"I do not." I said emphatically.

"No worry; none of us do. Come, have some punch." The gentleman was wearing black tails that made him appear tall and thin. He tipped his hat to me and turned toward the punch bowl. He dipped some of the pale, frothy liquid infused with rose petals. He smiled as he handed me the cup. I suddenly felt welcome.

"Your name is?"

"Beck…I mean Miss Beck."

"You don't say? Are you related to the Becks from the North?" He tapped his temple with his right index finger as though it helped him remember.

"No, my family is from the East."

"Are they in real estate," he inquired with a thick roll of his tongue on the r.

"No, they are in cattle."

"Well now, that is an admirable investment." I bowed my head and ducked away from him before any more questions came.

Out in the center of the room stood a remarkable figure of a woman with long dark hair that turned under in an easy style. She wore a simple gown of black velvet. I saw neither combs nor flowers. I walked her way. I stood back three feet for fear of infringing on her privacy. She was greeting guests from left and right. It was one of those scenes that remind you of a queen bee in her hive. Suddenly, it was my turn in line. I moved closer to her as she extended her hand. The closer I got, the uglier she appeared. Who was she? And why did Rosehill guests flock to her?

44

I'd better not ask too many questions. She extended her long gloved hand to me, pushing the thumb upward toward the fingers. It was her way of greeting—the delicate squeeze of the hand. She smiled a big toothy smile, and when she did, I could see she had uneven rows of teeth that looked like randomly stacked hay bales. Her chin became more elongated with the broad smile. Her gray eyes twinkled. And just then, I felt comfortable—like I'd met someone I knew—an old friend. Returning a smile, I said my name as though I were Royalty. "Miss Beck," ma'am.

"Do call me Marian."

"Marian, delighted to meet you."

"The sentiment is returned, my dear Miss Beck."

I heard a clearing of the throat behind me as another guest waited in line to greet the elegant lady draped in black. I stepped aside, regretting that there wasn't time for more of an introduction.

"Over here," said a female voice from the corner. "Yes, you! Do come and join us." She was ushering me over to socialize with her. Perfect! I could do some sleuthing.

"Thank you for inviting me over to join you. I'm Miss Beck. And you are?"

"I am Calista." Her hair was dark and radiant, and her eyes were wild like a gypsy's. She clearly had Spanish roots.

"What a lovely name! It sounds Spanish. Does your family come from Spain?"

"My name, my complexion, my hair and eyes give me away." She laughed out loud, slightly throwing her head back. Have you been to Spain, Miss Beck?"

"Not yet, Calista. But one day I would like to tour Spain and Portugal. I've been to France, Italy...."

She interrupted me. "Gigi is from France. Have you met her yet?" She pointed a finger toward the petite maid who had ushered me in through the ornate sitting room doors. "She is so much more than a maid. She is a lady's maid too. She sees to feathers in hats and fits the ladies for corsets. She irons and fluffs and stuffs— whatever is necessary to make us look grand."

"Yes, I noticed she fluffed my skirt at the door."

Calista looked down at my gown. "Miss Beck, you need a crinoline. Your gown is lovely, but it needs to stand out like Marian's. Gigi will fit you."

"Why must we all look like Marian?" Clearly I'd said something wrong because Calista shot a disturbed look my way.

"Marian is the fashion setter among us. Follow her lead, and you won't go wrong. She is often seen among men in black velvet. Women seldom wear black velvet, but Marian can make it seem perfectly appropriate. If she wore a cutaway coat, I dare say that we all would try it at least once."

I'd been warned. Marian was the belle here in the sitting room, and who knows where else she had clout.

"Do join us this evening for a reading, Miss Beck. Marian will be sharing a few pages from her new novel."

"Where? Here?"

"No, Miss Beck. This is the gathering room for socializing. Follow me, and I'll show you the library where Marian will be reading this evening." Calista stepped in front of me, walked with a decided pace through the lace draped French doors, and turned right into the hallway. "There it is. The door on the right at the end of the hall. I will meet you outside the library tonight at 8:00 P.M."

"Can I have a look at the library. I adore books!"

"Not now, Miss Beck. Guests can only occupy one room at a time. And of course you have your own room."

"What? Do you mean I can't walk down here to get a book at will?"

"No, Miss Beck. Do you have a first name?"

"Of course I have a first name, but I prefer to be called Miss Beck."

"Oh—I see. Did Miss Evans share her first name with you? Did I?"

I knew the way Calista responded that her Spanish temper was showing. I had insulted her by not trusting her with my full name. As of yet, I trusted no one here.

"Calista, I apologize if I have insulted you. You offered your name freely and so did Marian. Who is Miss Evans?"

"Miss Evans is Marian Evans the novelist. You've not heard of her?"

"No, I can't say that I have."

"And you are staying in the Eliot Room?"

"Yes."

"Oh dear." Somehow I'd failed a test for being well-informed on the premises. "I'll see you tonight. Don't be late to the library, MISS Beck." Calista walked away with her chin up and head thrown back. What a mess I'd made of things already.

I waited until she was out of sight, and pressed the library doors. They opened! I had committed some odd violation, but it felt wickedly right. I pushed on through the dark doors. There was a switch just inside that lit the central gas lamps, but it was not enough to reveal the rows of books in their entirety. Just those on the center shelves were faintly lit. I spotted more gas lights situated halfway up the walls between the shelves, and switched each one on. The gas smell and tiny smoke trails were oddly comforting.

All around the perimeter of the library—some six hundred square feet—I could see multi-colored leather volumes from floor to ceiling. Mesmerized, I ran my finger along a row of novels at eye level.

Snap! The side lights went out as though controlled by someone from outside the room. I ran to the door to let myself out before the central lights went out. The halls were empty. My heart raced like a trapped rabbit's. I somehow collected myself after a moment or two, and moved inconspicuously down the hallway toward the sitting room. The room was dark. The hall lights were dimming too. I began to run—back to the Eliot Room, back to the ghost cat that was somehow friendlier than this wing of the house.

I slid my skeleton key into the room lock. The heavy door fell open to a cozy room lit by a fireplace and candles. The room maid must have come in before sunset and started the fire for me. I dropped into one of the reading chairs, propping my feet on the delicate footstool. I looked at the boots I'd worn to the sitting room. No one had noticed. My height and the long skirt disguised the fact that I was not wearing formal button-up shoes. Drawing my hands to my lap to rest by the fire, I realized that I had one of the leather books from the back library shelf still clutched in my hand.

Now what? Another violation! No getting by with this bit of subterfuge. I'd entered the library without permission. What would the consequences be when Miss Brook found out?

I turned the book over to read the title on the front. *The Mill on the Floss* by George Eliot. It was the very one I wanted to read next. Just as I cracked the cover, there was a knock on the door.

"Ma'am?"

"Yes, you may enter." I shoved the book under my hip and waited for the maid to show herself.

"Would you like a tray in your room? Or would you like to go to the formal dining room?"

"A tray please, Miss Matthews. What is for dinner?"

"At your request, ma'am, we have ordered you a special meal tonight."

"Oh, good, I'm starving! What is tonight's meal?"

"Tea and toast, ma'am. Your favorite."

"For dinner?"

"The kitchen got word from Miss Brook that you ate nothing on your breakfast tray except toast and tea. Perhaps you will be hungry enough to eat your British breakfast in the morning?"

"Sure, tea and toast is fine."

"There's marmalade too, ma'am."

"Thank you."

When the room maid disappeared behind my door, I heaped orange marmalade onto the toast wedges and ate greedily. After three cups of tea, I finally felt like my stomach was satisfied. If only Mr. Cooper were here. I could get an order of anything I wanted—even biscuits and gravy! How had I missed my lunch? Perhaps they came when I was soaking in the tub.

I pulled the book into view and began to examine it. It had a finely tooled leather spine, and the pages were sewn between two sturdy marbleized book boards. The initials "G.E." were stamped in gold leaf script on the front. I read the first chapter and felt right at home. The author was adept at setting a mood. I almost felt homesick for country houses, hay ricks, cows, and corn after reading the introduction describing the Griff house and property.

The regulator clock over the fireplace mantle struck 7:00 P.M. I rushed to the wardrobe to find the perfect gown to wear into the library. Should I wear black velvet? Why not? I was meeting Marian Evans, novelist, tonight.

The Library

Chapter 9

I checked my appearance in the floor length mirror. I looked dramatic and mysterious in the black velvet gown darted at the waistline. The frock was placed prominently in the wardrobe, its hanger protruding from the knob of wood hangers that were stacked upon one another to the back of the antiquated closet. On the floor of the wardrobe near the black gown was a pair of low black heels. On the toe of the shoe was a miniature embroidered gold fleur de lis. They would have to do. I couldn't wear the ivory boots tonight because I had to sit down to listen to Miss Evans. Surely if the pale boots were discovered underneath my black velvet gown, it would be considered faux pas.

The regulator clock struck 7:45 P.M. I made my way out of the room, grabbing a few flowers from the hall table vase to tuck into my hair. I was new at this, but also willing to play the part. The snowy Stephanotis blossoms were dainty and fragrant. So feminine.

"Good evening, Miss Beck." Miss Brook was making her way down the hall to summon me to the library. "How was your evening meal?"

"Lovely." I lied.

"We're serving hors d'oeuvres in the library, ma'am."

"Oh good! I've heard so much about your socials, and your hors d'oeuvres, I hear, are to die for."

"A pretty lady like you with such intellectual curiosity must have attended many socials."

"I am not a socialite, Miss Brook. I'm not anti-social, but I prefer my private time. Most parties present a waste of time for me. You see...." She stopped me in mid-sentence and opened the door to the library.

"We'll talk more later, Miss Beck. Good evening."

Inside the library, Calista was making rounds. I walked to meet her. She was wearing a red satin gown embellished in black lace, and in her hair was a large black comb that held her upswept hair in place. She was stunning.

"Calista! Good evening."

"Ah, Miss Beck, I was about to go to the door to greet you, but the library grandfather clock had not yet chimed 8:00 P.M."

"Miss Brook came for me and walked me down to the library."

"That was kind of her. Since this is your first night in the library. You will be introduced to the entire Rosehill guest family."

"Oh, I was not aware. I'm a bit shy."

"Do tell? And that black velvet gown you are wearing is questionable, Miss Beck."

"Questionable? What do you mean? I thought you said Miss Evans liked black velvet."

"She does—look!" My eyes scanned the room. There she was in a stunning black velvet gown which fell in folds to the floor, the bodice was smocked, and the sleeves were short and simple. Her hands were long and slender. They needed no ornamentation. Her chestnut hair was loose, but she was wearing a black lace mantilla which disguised her facial features. I scanned the room again, taking in the scene for a few seconds. Only Miss Evans and I were dressed in black velvet. The gods were against me!

"I've committed another faux pas! I'd better go change."

"Too late now, Miss Beck." In the background the grandfather clock chimed eight times. The guests found their seats quickly, balancing hors d'oeuvres and flutes of champagne on their laps.

"Everyone—everyone, please be seated. Miss Evans will be reading momentarily," came a booming voice from the center of the room.

"What is Miss Evans reading this evening, Calista?"

"She is reading a few chapters from *The Mill on the Floss.*"

"Why is she reading from someone else's book? Didn't George Eliot write *The Mill on the Floss?*"

"Oh, dear, Miss Beck, you do need to catch up with the times."

"What do you mean?" Before Calista could answer, a peacock of a lady with a hat in full plume walked to the back wall of the library and searched the shelf at eye level. She seemed puzzled. She looked again, then turned. She walked back to the center of the room, and announced that the George Eliot novel was missing. The room went silent. All of the social chatter that had been circling like smoke rings now ceased, and all eyes were on the peacock—even Miss Evans' head was angled toward her, listening intently.

"I can't explain it. The book was there earlier today." The door to the library flew open, and in rushed Miss Brook. She handed a book to Miss Evans and turned to reassure the guests that *The Mill on the Floss* had been found. She shot a look my way. My knees felt week as she stepped back to the door where the room maid, Miss Matthews, was waiting.

I'd been ratted out! The rooms had been searched. Mine was particularly suspect since I'd been in the library without permission. Someone knew I was in there alone. They switched the lights out on me earlier that evening. I was toast!

"It was you," Calista said. "I'm sure you have a perfectly reasonable explanation, Miss Beck. I am happy to hear you out."

"Yes, it was. I came here earlier today. I just had to have a look. When I stepped inside, I felt like I'd entered a womb. I had just begun to run my finger over that very row of books at the back of the room when the entrance lights were switched off on me."

"Serves you right, MISS Beck. Womb?" Sheepishly I left her side and found a seat in the corner. Calista remained with a group of guests with whom she seemed comfortable.

All eyes turned toward Miss Evans as she lifted the book and gently opened it to where I'd left the marker—oh no! I'd put the numbered room key in the book to mark my place. She looked at me, and I could see her rows of smiling teeth through the black lace veil. She knew.

"Good evening, Rosehill guests. I've decided to read a random page this evening from my new novel, *The Mill on the Floss*. As most of you know, this story is based on my life at Griff."

Say what? Her book; her life? I must have heard her wrong. Whatever the case, she was on to me, and there was no escaping a future conversation regarding the matter of the missing book. I took a huge gulp of my champagne, and sat back with my eyes closed. I could absorb the reading better that way.

Miss Evans read one page and closed the book. Everyone stood to offer a round of applause. As I stood to join them, my champagne spilled.

"Miss Beck, would you sit with me?" came the soft river-like voice of Miss Evans. I fumbled for my linen napkin to wipe my gown.

"Me, Miss Evans?"

"You are the only Miss Beck in the room, yes?"

"Yes, Miss Evans. I believe so."

"Then come here, and sit next to me."

I noticed that Miss Evans rarely invited one person in the room to sit with her. Typically the guests were introduced to her by some little man dressed in black. What was she doing with him? He didn't seem her type at all. Maybe he was just one of her servants. But his hair was greasy like he'd overdone the barbershop pomade. He looked familiar—like I'd met him elsewhere.

"Miss Evans, forgive me for taking the book. It was an accident. You see, I entered the library without permission. It was inviting—like a womb."

"Womb? I do like that description of a library, Miss Beck. Are you a writer?"

"I'm a journalist, Miss Evans. In my work, I don't have much call for using flowery metaphors, but I do have a command of the English language." Miss Evans smiled at me through her veil.

"That was my beginning. I wrote articles and reviews

for the *Westminster Review* in London."

"You are from London, Marian?"

"I have lived in London, but it is not my home. My real home is in Warwickshire, at the Griff house. Have you been to England, Miss Beck?"

"I regret to say I have not, though I do have friends from Devon who have invited me to tea."

"Devonshire is lovely, Miss Beck. You should go. The coastline is like no other. And Bath is just a few days north by carriage. The hot springs are excellent for aches and pains. You might also consider the Wiltshire Plains. Do you care for mysteries? If so, you will love the powerful Stonehenge site."

"I've never really thought about it, Miss Evans. But I guess I do like mysteries. I'm a natural sleuth."

"Do call me Marian."

"Marian." I repeated.

"Sit down and we will chat for a time." She patted her long slender fingers on the overstuffed lounge.

"I'm so honored, Marian."

"It is I who am honored, Miss Beck."

"Do call me Sara."

"I love the name Sara in all of its variety of spellings. I had a friend named Sara once."

The short man with the unkempt hair joined us at Marian's right side. "Marian, dear, the other guests wish to spend time with you too."

"Of course, George. I will say good evening to you then, Sara. It was so nice getting to know one another. See you again soon."

"It was delightful, Marian. Good evening." I nodded my head to her and to the tiny man in black who had come between us.

The chimes on the hall clock melodically played ten bells, and as it echoed down the hall, the guests watched the door. A shadow appeared outside the lace curtained windows. A key inserted in the lock turned. The door opened to reveal Miss Brook.

"The reading is over for this evening. You may return to your rooms." She shot a look my way as I walked toward the door. "I'm watching you, Beck."

"I'm sorry, Miss Brook. I was only borrowing the book. I would have returned it. Honest."

Through narrowed lips, Miss Brook uttered words I would never forget. "You trespassed! You took Miss Evans' book without asking. Do you believe in karma, Miss Beck?"

"Karma—well, maybe. I'm not sure I believe all that nonsense. It is similar to superstition and wives' tales. We live in the modern world, Miss Brook."

"No maybes about karma, Miss Beck. You brought about the actions, and now they will return to teach you a lesson." She ushered me through the door and watched as I walked around the corner to my room.

I felt frightened for the first time in years. Miss Brook seemed a bit creepy. I walked hurriedly to my room. The door was standing ajar. I stepped inside and bolted the door. Just then I remembered my room key, used as a bookmark for *The Mill on the Floss*, now in Miss Evans' possession! I could bolt the door from the inside, but if I left my room, it would be unlocked for the world to come in and snoop. This—this is why I have had the same apartment for years—stay to myself—regulate everything around me to keep the world at bay. I desperately needed to be in control of my environment. I slid a chair under the door knob.

Restless Partners
Dream

Chapter 10

"George, perhaps we could make our way to the Wiltshire Plains today. I'd love to see Stonehenge and Avebury. You do know that Emerson made his way to Stonehenge? I'm sure I've told you before, but when I was young and spending most of my time soaking up sensible literature with the Brays at Rosehill, I met him—Emerson that is. What an amazing man—'the first man I'd ever seen.' He expressed himself with dignity, intelligence, sensibility."

"Tell me, dear Marian, did you enjoy his company more than mine?" The small greasy-haired man moved to Marian's side and leaned to kiss her on the cheek.

"Seriously? I could never love another as I love you, George."

"More than Emerson? More than Spencer? More than Durad who used his own facial features and added your hair and décolletage to paint that flattering picture of you in that soft black drawstring velvet gown?"

"Oh, George, stop teasing me. You are the only one who ever loved me for my body as well as my mind. You are the only one who overlooked my face long enough to find my heart and soul."

"My Marian…my darling devoted girl."

"Yes, I am, George. I wish you would remember that when you go off to London with your literary fellows, drinking brandy and smoking cigars through the night. I need you here with me. The halls echo with the ticking and chiming of the clocks, but they are not happy echoes—they remind me of your absence. They remind me of the loss of so many in my life. I fear someday I will lie in our bed alone."

"My pet, don't create illusions in your mind. They are fine for characters in your popular novels, but they are not reflective of our relationship. We are linked, Marian. We are linked like no one can or ever will be again. Soul-linked, my dear. Come, let's go to bed now, and remind ourselves of this treasure."

"Oh George, you do calm me and my silly fears. I would love to go into the city with you—to sit with you for tea, hold your hand, and watch as admirers pass and tip their hats at you."

"Marian, we've been over this before. I'm a married man. I cannot subject you to the prattle of high society."

"I don't care about that!"

"Yes, you do—you care about it more than most. Now come with me, and let's forget these silly notions. I will always be here—always." His eyes softened her, his words soothed her, his masculine air of protection suited her.

George took Marian's hand and guided her carefully to the dark bedroom that smelled of old books, brandy, and clove oil. "This is the story of our lives, Marian—this home, our walls of books, the busts of German philosophers, our full snifters of brandy, the collection of paintings and photographs in the drawing room, especially that one of you in the...." Marian stopped him short and pulled him into the dense bed. "Oh, Marian, you still have your booties on!" He reached to remove her delicate ivory boots one by one. She sighed as he moved up beside her between the sheets.

"Poetry, George?"

"Now?" He looked bewildered.

"Yes, please. Read to me, dearest."

"What would you like most to hear?"

"Wordsworth."

"Not Emerson?"

"Oh, George! There was nothing between Emerson and me but a play and a night full of philosophy. Besides, the word in the circuit had it that he was still in love with his first wife who died shortly after they were married. He nearly lost his mind over her. I heard he remarried."

"That Emerson was a busy man. How did he manage to have time for writing and travel?"

"There was this other lady he was quite fond of too. What was her name? Oh—that's right—Margaret, that philosophical female muse that walked among the Transcendentalist men in the States. She was brilliant and beautiful, I've heard. Lydian Emerson, his second wife, must have been jealous." Poor woman—torn at both ends: the first wife's ghost and the ghost of Margaret Fuller who died tragically in a shipwreck with her husband and baby."

George fidgeted for their worn volume of William Wordworth's poetry on the nightstand. He flipped the pages open to a random poem and began to read to Marian.

> Beneath these fruit-tree boughs that shed
> Their snow-white blossoms on my head,
> With brightest sunshine round me spread
> Of spring's unclouded weather,
> In this sequestered nook how sweet
> To sit upon my orchard-seat!
> And birds and flowers once more to greet,
> My last year's friends together.

"That's The Green Linnet poem! I know it well. How melodious Wordsworth's words. He is a literary master of mood." Marian swooned from her side of the bed.

"Are you swooning over Wordsworth now, Marian?"

"Never more than you, George. Come here—put the book away."

"While you are in your Wordsworth mood, I'd better turn down the lamp." Marian giggled and moved close to him. They sank to the center of the large Victorian bed.

The Visitor

Chapter 11

My mouth was dry, and my head felt like an attic full of cobwebs. I sat up in bed to get my wits about me. The sun was peeping through brocade curtains at the west windows. Beyond the window sill, farmer Newburne's sheep were grazing on a sloping hill behind the Rosehill B & B. It was a scene right out of a travel book of England—Dorset perhaps, or maybe Devon.

My heart was not in the moment as I willed myself out of bed. I was feeling diminished by Miss Brook and her confrontational manner with me the night before. I stepped into the ivory boots. Suddenly the room began to spin. The champagne from the library soiree! Running to the bathroom, I dry-heaved for several moments. It produced nothing, but a painful stomach.

"Ma'am, I have your breakfast!" The maid was waiting at my door. I rushed to let her in. I was anxious for toast and tea even at the prospect of vomiting it up.

"Good morning!" She stepped into the room, setting a full tray of British breakfast on the table between the reading chairs.

"Thank you! I could use some nourishment. But wait—not just toast and tea?"

"Would you like a tray in your room for lunch, ma'am?"

"Yes, please. I would prefer not to socialize today. I feel like such a fool having borrowed that book without asking. I didn't know it was Miss Evan's own copy!"

"Oh, ma'am, I wouldn't take it too seriously. It is a lesson learned. Just let it go. Besides, Miss Evans has many books on that library shelf."

"Do tell?" There was a knock from the hallway side of the door. The maid answered it. Miss Brook stood with her hands on her hips. By the sour look on her face, she was not happy!

"Miss Matthews, there are other guests to be served!"

"Sorry, Miss Brook." The maid curtsied and let herself out of the room.

"So, will you be going down to the dining room today, or would you like a lunch tray brought to your room?" Miss Brook questioned.

"A tray in my room please."

"Hmmm…" came a curious wordless judgment from Miss Brook's throat. She turned and let herself out. I bolted the door behind her. I felt ten years old again, and my mother was scolding me for not doing my chores and helping with my younger sisters. My childhood room had been my hiding place.

My stomach felt sick again. The sudden memory jolt back to my childhood had not helped. I ran to the bathroom, retching as I went. After my stomach was emptied, I sipped tea and nibbled toast wedges. Anything else and I would be in the bathroom all day. I hid a fresh pear in my purse for later.

I needed to hear from someone who cared about me—someone outside this crazy house. The only name that occurred to me was Mr. Cooper. I pulled my purse up from the floor. What day was this? Was Cat OK? I should ask Mr. Cooper to check on him. I couldn't ask my neighbor Jenny because I'd just sent her packing from my house. I dialed Mr. Cooper's direct number at work.

"Mr. Cooper!" came the familiar blustery voice.

"Oh, Mr. Cooper, you're there!"

"Where else would I be, Beck? Where are you?"

"At this insane Rosehill place. I know—don't laugh. I drove back here after we spoke at lunch, and tried to return the book I'd borrowed. But the daffy maid said there was a storm brewing, and farmer Newburne had long-since taken the sheep down to their pens. There was lightning. She made it sound as though I had no choice but to stay and continue my experience."

"Daffy maid? That doesn't sound like you, Beck. That sounds like me!" He laughed until he started himself coughing. He went silent for a moment, probably tipping back in his chair, lighting a cigar.

"Oh, Mr. Cooper, if I were there I'd smoke a cigar with you!"

"You would?"

"Yes. I'm so miserable."

"You, the full of control—nobody breaks through my barrier—Beck?"

"I know, and I should just calm down, pack up and leave. But there is something about this place that has drawn me in. I don't fit in at all, and I'm supposed to be having an experience—learning something. The other guests have no problem living here and abiding by the house rules."

"And you, Beck?"

"I've committed several violations."

"Like what?"

"I sneaked into the library without asking permission, and borrowed a book. The maid found it in my room, and all hell broke loose."

"That's it? I did worse things in kindergarten, Beck!"

"You did?"

"Would I lie?"

"Probably!"

"What else happened, Beck? You've come unwound."

"Well, I wore a black velvet dress that was hanging in my wardrobe, and when I arrived at the library for the evening reading, Calista—she's the Spanish lady that made friends with me first—said I should not have worn the black velvet dress that evening because Miss Evans—Marian—was wearing her black velvet dress that evening."

"Who in the hell does Miss Evans think she is? And is Calista the social monitor of Rosehill?"

"Well, yes, Calista is the fashion advisor. That is—she and Gigi, the French maid."

"Spanish fashion advisor and a French maid? Were you at a masquerade ball?"

"No, Mr. Cooper. Everyone dresses for afternoon punch in the sitting room. And at 8:00 P.M. we gather in the library for a reading. Miss Evans read last night."

"Tell me more about this Evans chick."

"Marian has written her own books, but she prefers to read books written by George Eliot instead of reading her own aloud. She is a friendly person. And powerfully ugly."

"Powerfully ugly? And loves George Eliot novels. Hmmm?" I could almost hear his synapses firing!

"Mr. Cooper, are you still there?"

"Yes, Beck. Something is not quite right there. I'll be right over."

"No, Mr. Cooper, I need to handle this on my own. I do need to ask a favor of you though. Would you get into my desk at work, and get my apartment key at the back of the drawer? It's hidden inside a Bazooka gum wrapper. Please go to my apartment and see if my cat, Cat is all right."

"You have a cat named Cat? That took some imagination! Look, Beck, I can help, but it won't be until this evening. We're close to deadline now."

"OK, Mr. Cooper. Please call me back as soon as you can. My phone battery is almost dead, and there is no charger here. I'd have to sit outside in my car to recharge my phone. I can bet that is another violation of sorts!"

"Talk with you later then. Should I send a cake with a saw blade baked inside?"

"Mr. Cooper!" He laughed and coughed at the same time. Then he was gone. For the first time in my adult life, I felt needy. Mr. Cooper seemed a tower of strength instead of his usual obnoxious self. Had he changed, or had I?"

I placed my phone back into my purse, and returned to the bathroom. Running a full tub of water, I leaned back, dreaming of my apartment, the sound of Michael Buble's voice meandering through my kitchen, and Cat.

I awoke with a start when I heard a soft knock at the door. I put on a robe and stepped to the door. "Who is it?"

"It is Marian, Sara."

"Oh, uh, I'm dripping from the tub. Wait just a moment. I dried my feet and put on the soft boots so I would not mark the floor. Then I opened the door.

"Forgive me Miss Evans. Do come in."

"No worry, Sara. Would you like to come down to lunch with me?"

"Oh, Marian, I'm sorry, I've already ordered a tray."

"Then I shall order a tray too, and eat with you. It is all right if I invite myself to your lovely Eliot Room?"

"Yes, indeed."

"Here is your room key, my dear." She handed over the skeleton key marked #1 Eliot Room.

"What a fool I made of myself last night: wearing the black velvet dress, taking the very book you needed for your reading, spilling my champagne."

"We are all here to learn, Sara. Experience it, and let it go. Laugh at the little things. No one can always be in control. This house is full of trickery. You must be willing to laugh when the house laughs."

"When the house laughs?"

"Yes, Sara. When I was young, my family lived in a tall, brick manor house called Griff. There was so much work to do all day long—indoors and out. The chickens needed fed, eggs needed gathering, the cheese and butter-making took up the better part of an afternoon. We cooked huge evening meals for our family and the farmhands. But at night, I swear the house laughed when my family gathered at the front fireplace near Father's office. I read Sir Walter Scott's *Waverly*, and everyone marveled at how well I read.

"It sounds so idyllic, Marian. Tell me more."

"Let us sit down first, my dear."

"Yes, sit here in one of the reading chairs."

"Thank you, Sara. Oh—what is this?" She'd sat on a book that I'd tucked into the chair cushion. We both laughed aloud, and I swear the house was laughing with us—at least the room where we sat—two friends who needed one another at that moment in time.

"You see, my dear, it is nothing. It is a silly borrowed book, and little more. You can carry it back to the library later. There will be no trouble. Right now, we will talk and share."

Marian lifted the book to see the title. Her face brightened as she ran her fingers over the gilt letters on the marbleized cover of *Adam Bede*.

"I wish it had been one of my first reads, Marian. I did not know of your work in high school because I was such a tomboy. I read Steinbeck novels back to back. Do you know John Steinbeck, Marian?" I dropped into the chair beside her.

"Lovely," she said admiring the ivory boots that revealed themselves when I sat down. "May I try them on?"

"Please do. They were here in this room when I first came. I thought they were too small for me, but when I slipped them on, they fit perfectly." I handed the warm boots over to Marian.

"Oh, how lovely, almost like butter." She removed her black button-up shoes and slid the boots on with ease.

"They fit you perfectly too!"

"Yes, my dear, they do." Marian put her feet up on the footstool and leafed through *Adam Bede*. "I do not know John Steinbeck's work. Tell me about him. Perhaps he is new?"

"No, he's an award-winning novelist, Marian. I'm surprised you have not heard of him."

"But then again, you had not heard of me until you came to Rosehill."

"Touche'!" We laughed—full-throated laughs that startled the room maid when she knocked.

"Come in."

"Is everything all right, ma'am?" She saw Miss Evans in the chair beside me. "Oh, I fear Miss Brook will not approve of this arrangement." She hung her head as though she did not want to see any more.

"Miss Matthews, there is no arrangement, only two friends sharing lunch. Will you be so kind as to bring me a tray too? Miss Beck is not feeling well today, and I will sit with her to share lunch and conversation. Then I will return to my room."

The maid curtsied and walked out into the hall. The footsteps ceased for a moment. Marian and I laughed again, and the maid's footsteps continued down through the darkness toward the kitchen.

Evening to Remember

Chapter 12

"I do love an English breakfast, Sara. Don't you?" Marian ate like a lady, but one who was very hungry. "George is waiting for me to join him for breakfast too." I knew George Lewes had something to do with her anxiety about the time.

"I like toast, tea, and fruit." I fished the hidden pear out of my purse. Marian broke into a huge toothy smile. With each of her smiles came warmth, and soon I found her beauty beyond the rows of large, crooked teeth.

"Whatever suits you, dear, but remember you must keep your complexion and hair lovely, and a variety of foods goes a long way toward extending your youthful appearance. Now, I must go. Thank you for sharing breakfast and conversation with me. Will you join me in the library this evening?"

"I would love to, Marian. See you then."

"Oh, and don't wear the house booties with your silk gown, my dear." She was laughing as she let herself out. I shook my head and closed the door. I felt a huge smile on my face. I had just had a private conversation with a novelist. She was not just a novelist; she was a social icon—a trendsetter. How could I be so blessed?

I missed the sitting room experience in the afternoon, and no one came with a lunch tray for me, though I'd asked for one. Clearly, I was not favored among the guests. I was the rebel who would not quietly enjoy my experience and follow the house rules. I felt like the young boy in *The Giver*, a young adult book I'd read many years ago. What he went through to stand against the status quo!

Looking around the room to find some kind of food, I noticed that the *Adam Bede* novel was left open to a particular page. I began to read.

> While she adjusted the broad leaves that set off the pale fragrant butter as the primrose is set off by its nest of green, I am afraid Hetty was thinking a great deal more of the looks Captain Donnithorne had cast at her than of Adam and his troubles.

My head began to spin in a déjà vu sort of way. I lay down on the bed, pulling the book up beside me. I closed my eyes and was transported—not to sleep—but to a remembrance that was like a dream. Was I dreaming, soul traveling, channeling, remembering something I'd read?

A young lady with dark curly hair is patting butter in the dairy, humming as she uses the butter paddle to shape the loaves of fresh creamery butter. Her hair is held back by a white mushroom cap, and her simple cotton gypsy blouse reveals her fine figure. Any visitor might notice that she is happy at her station. She could be elsewhere, but she is here.

A sandy-haired man enters and bids her good morning. She turns, shyly smiles, and returns the greeting as she continues to form the butter and weigh it on the scale. The persistent visitor inquires about the butter maid's afternoon schedule. She politely tells him that she is learning lace work at a neighbor's house. His eyes twinkle. Her cheeks turn red.

I sat up in bed, realizing that I wanted to be that woman with the dark curly hair. I wanted the man to be taken with me—with my looks, my shy way, my simple joy of country living.

What was happening to me? Was I missing my ex, and fantasizing about two lovers I didn't know? Was I acting out the part of Hetty—bringing the characters to life? I needed to know!

I was not doing myself any favors staying in my room so much, not going to every social gathering like the others were. But my need for privacy was woven into my nature like a little pocket full of treasures that I did not wish to share with anyone else.

I closed my eyes again, and lay my head back, nestling in like I were about to take the journey of my life. I wanted to see the sandy-haired man again. I desired to smell the fresh butter and shape it in my own hands. I needed to feel the warm blush of my cheeks as the young man stood in the doorway smiling at me. I needed to be loved. And after a time, there was the sandy-haired man standing in the doorway of the dairy, his bright blue eyes flashing like warning beacons at the young butter maid.

The young man asks about the child he had seen before on a visit to the dairy farm. The dark-haired girl says she is at the house. Her name is Totty. He asks what the butter maid's name is. She replies modestly, "My name is Hetty." He says the name himself and seems to like it. It suits her in her simple setting. He tells her he may see her on one of her walks to the neighboring farm. Her face comes alive with hope as she knows like every woman knows that they will meet again soon. The dairy room darkens as the scene ends.

Who were these people? Was I fantasizing? Perhaps I was being given the pages of a novel I was to write. Had a benevolent being led me there to that time and place so that I could fulfill my writing dreams? The regulator clock struck seven chimes. I had been dreaming, or fantasizing for hours.

The wardrobe stood across the room begging to be opened. Each time there was a new experience—new clothes, new shoes, new hats. Who was providing these things? I took the double door knobs with both hands and opened the doors with a swish. I gasped when I saw a pale blue silk dress hanging in front with matching shoes on the floor of the closet. I pulled the garment down from the clothes hook and held it up to my body. It was exquisite! I tried on the gown with the excitement of a teenager preparing for prom. Every curve was accentuated. I'd never worn such a gorgeous gown in all my life. The shoes were the perfect complement. Just then I remembered what Marian had said about not wearing house booties with my blue silk gown tonight. She knew!

I reached for my phone to call Mr. Cooper before things got any crazier for me. My phone was dead. I was on my own now with no Mr. Cooper to bail me out. I pinned my hair and placed silver combs above each ear. I looked at myself in the floor length mirror. It was an unbelievable transformation! Not my usual taupe or tan or cream, but I adored the feminine look and feel of the silk. I was feeling the part of a lady too after that dream or fantasy or remembrance—whatever it was that brought my senses alive.

I found a fine lace shawl thrown over the back of the fainting couch, draped it over my shoulders, and headed for the door. I walked slowly, hoping to see some of the guests leaving their rooms. I wanted to get a peek inside, curious to know what experiences they were having—too curious for my own good.

I walked the length of the hall and turned right to pass the sitting room, then around the corner to the library. The doors were closed, but the lights were on. I waited. The hall clock struck eight chimes before I dared enter. The door opened from the inside. Gigi smiled broadly at me. "Mademoiselle, I love your gown, and those shoes." She almost blushed with excitement.

"I'm glad you like them, Gigi. It was the first thing I found in the closet tonight." I winked at her and moved on. There were several guests gathered at the back of the library who were chattering and nodding their heads about something. I walked closer to hear their conversation.

"I cannot imagine what she must be thinking!" one heavy-set lady said as she drew a hand to her cheek, expressing shock.

"Nor I!" came from the thinning lips of an older woman who was dressed in light pink organza. Her gray hair needed no hat or bow or even flowers. It was strikingly beautiful like fresh snow in moonlight.

A man wearing a top hat and tails spoke up, "Ladies, I do think you are making much of nothing. Miss Evans is allowed to visit anyone she wishes whether it be the lady who lodges in the Room #1, or the little greasy-haired man in black who follows her like a devoted pug."

Was I hearing this conversation correctly? The heavy-set lady noticed me listening in, her eyes widened, and she put a finger up to her lips to signal the others.

"Have I committed another violation?"

"Oh no," spoke the man, stepping forward and removing his top hat to greet me.

"You were eavesdropping," said the elderly woman in the pink organza. "This conversation was none of your business."

"It is my business if you are talking about me!" I turned and walked away hurriedly. I heard mumbling behind me as I drifted off to another group of guests, Calista among them. She was enchanting in her red lace dress that fell in folds to the floor.

"Calista!"

"Oh, Miss Beck, come join us. Bravo!" Calista cheered. "Come, Mr. Lewes, meet Miss Beck. Miss Beck—Mr. George Lewes. Mr. Lewes—Miss Beck." I noticed the bossy companion of Marian's was at the center of the group. He was speaking in French. He looked like an animated actor on a stage speaking his lines.

"Good to see you, Miss Beck. I believe we met last evening?"

"Not exactly, Mr. Lewes, you spoke to Marian, not me. But I am happy to be formally introduced to you now. I do admire Marian. I enjoyed my breakfast with her this morning."

"Yes, about that...."

Marian interrupted Mr. Lewes before he made a fool of himself. "My dear Sara, let us excuse ourselves from this group and walk along the library shelves together. We must select a book for this evening's reading." She took my arm in the crook of hers, and led me along the back wall of the library where the novels were kept.

"I do so love books. Don't you, Sara? I should say I love books more than just about anything. They are my passion. I carry them everywhere I go. Well, George carries them, and of course our movers. When we travel, we take trunks of them with us. Our first trip together was to Weimer. Have you been to Germany, Sara?"

"No, I have not, Marian. I would love to see the Black Forest."

"Then we should travel together back to Germany. George won't mind."

Just then George stepped up behind us to usher Marian to the center of the room. I felt like a discarded dance card. There was something I did not like about George. Was it the way he managed her? Were they in love? Did they live together? Did they only travel together? Perhaps he was her manager? In any case, George would not want me poking along with them as they toured foreign countries.

"Sara, do come here, and sit beside me."

"Yes, Marian." I walked to her, handing her the book she'd slipped into my hand before George so rudely interrupted us.

"*Romola*, this is Calista's favorite." Marian divided the pages and began to read. Calista drew near and stood at my side. Her dark shining eyes were full of wonder and adventure. She placed her hand on my arm, and gave a light squeeze.

Along the back wall surrounding the hors d'oeuvres and champagne flutes stood the gossip mongers who had insulted me earlier. I scanned the room to see who else had attended. A young man with sandy brown hair was standing at the far end of the library close to the doors. He was tall and handsome. His eyes were surveying the room, but he seemed to take no notice of us. I whispered to Calista, "Who is that striking young man over there?"

"That's a new guest, Miss Beck. He just checked in this evening. He's a little shy. We do not yet know his name."

"My name is Sara."

"What?" said Calista.

"Sara—my name is Sara, Calista." She squeezed my arm again as we shared a smile. "I must meet that man."

"Yes, you must," Calista returned, leveling her eyes to get a better look at the young gentleman. "I will speak with him on your behalf."

A Long Night

Chapter 13

I watched as the hands on the huge grandfather clock moved from 8:30 to 9:30 P.M. The sandy-haired gentleman sat down in a seat near the door. He was writing in a notebook. Perhaps he was a journalist too. I wondered why Calista had not yet approached him. It was getting late. I put on my best "approachable" look and walked over to introduce myself. As soon as he saw me coming, he dashed through the library doors and into the hall.

"That was odd behavior!" Calista was watching the whole scene. "I was asking around about him. No one knows him. Some say they don't think he is a registered guest. Very odd behavior indeed. I'd steer clear if I were you, Sara."

"Perhaps you are right, Calista." I was shivering inside. An avalanche of ice had just fallen on me once again. This young man had triggered it with his cool response to my approach. The jilt from my ex was still too fresh for such a snub. I bid Marian good night and started for the door. George hoofed up behind me, and addressed me as though he'd known me for years.

"My dear Sara, Marian has spoken to me of your conversations about reading, writing, and travel. She would like you—that is we would like you to join us when we travel later this week."

"Oh, Mr. Lewes, I would love that. Wait a moment, I have to travel to England later this week. I'm sorry."

"Let's all begin our journey in England together then. Who better to show you around than two Brits?"

"My goodness, just a week ago my boss pressed me to travel to England to check out some timeshares for him. He knew I needed time away. Now this invitation from Marian and you! Perhaps England is my destiny?"

"Your employer is?"

"Oh, sorry, I work for *The Times Herald* newspaper here in the city. My boss is the editor, Mr. Cooper."

"And your position at *The Times Herald*?"

"Investigative journalist."

"Oh, I see. Is Marian aware of this?"

"Yes. Is there a problem?"

"On the contrary. I just want to make sure Marian knows what she is getting herself into. You see, so many newspapers are trying to pinch a story on Marian. She uses a pseudonym to protect herself in public, but here she has used her real name. At any rate, we will be leaving on Friday if you would like to join us, Sara. You know, Marian once had a good friend in a talented young lady named Sara. Sara Hennell. Until tomorrow evening then." Without hesitation, George walked back to Marian.

Did I like him, or did I only tolerate him because of Marian? For some reason, I felt as though he was not being fair to her. She was writing and earning the paycheck while he strutted around the drawing rooms, parlors, and libraries holding her puppet strings. Perhaps I was being too judgmental—a knee-jerk first impression.

I entered the hall hoping to see the sandy-haired gentleman again. Yes, he had been rude, but I wanted to know him—the why of him. Specifically I wanted to know why he had dashed away when I approached. After all, I was stunning in my blue silk gown, and he was a wallflower. He needed to learn etiquette—Rosehill etiquette. Did I just say that?

My room was warm and cozy when I returned. My bed had been changed, and fresh towels hung on the heater next to the copper tub. I dared not open the wardrobe and spoil my surprise for tomorrow. I set my gloves on the end of the bed and noticed a letter with my name penned on the front in beautiful fountain pen script. I swept it up, my heart pounding like horses' hooves. It was from Marian.

"My dear Sara, I have spoken to George so that you might join us in travel on Friday. He will be speaking with you further about this. It is late, so for now I bid you goodnight. Your Marian."

I was breathless. Here was an invitation in her own hand! I dropped back onto the bed and kicked my feet with happiness. I was going to England! There was a huge cracking sound. The bed sank to the floor!

Immediately there were footsteps in the hall. Doors were opening, and voices began speaking all at once.

"Miss Beck, are you all right?" came the excited voice of the room maid.

"Yes—I just broke the bed is all."

"Oh dear. Can you open the door please."

"Coming...." I pulled myself out of the sunken bed and ran to the door.

"Now what, Miss Beck?" came the voice of a frustrated Miss Brook who was standing behind the maid. She stepped out and revealed her nightgown and sleeping cap. I could not keep from laughing.

"Restrain yourself, Miss Beck. There is nothing funny about reducing furniture to rubble, and waking the guests and staff at all hours!"

"I'm sorry, Miss Brook. It was an accident. I sat down on the bed too hard, and down it went."

"I see." She looked around the room to be sure there was no one of the opposite persuasion with me.

"No, Miss Brook, I do not have a lover in my room!" At that exclamation, all of the concerned guests in the hallway began to laugh. Miss Brook retreated through the door, stomping up the hallway.

"We'll fix it in the morning. Lesson learned; you'll have to sleep in the broken bed tonight." said the defeated Miss Brook.

"May we come in?" asked a handful of guests who had been listening in the hall.

"Dare we?" I questioned.

"Why not?" They rushed through the door which I held open quite far until they had all jammed in.

"What to hell is this place? Where are we?" asked a man dressed in late 1930s style clothing. He was bent forward as though he had a bad back.

"What do you mean, sir?"

"I mean—where are you in your experience—the 1800s? Look at this place! What books and authors did you choose?"

"I didn't. The book was here when I arrived. George Eliot is the author. I haven't had much chance to read, but here it is, *Adam Bede*."

"How can you stand it in here? It is damp and dark, and it smells of cloves?" said a shrill voice near the door. "And that cat has got to go; no pets allowed here!" The lady, who seemed to be the wife of the man, had seen the ghost cat, Tabby!

"You see the cat? No one else has seen Tabby."

"Cat? I don't see a cat," said the man who spoke first. "They put you in a haunted room, Miss!"

"It isn't haunted. It was previously occupied." I explained. The maid told me Tabby had died in the kitchen of this house, but the owner, a female, allowed the cat in this room. I saw it myself the second night here."

"Oh, the daffy maid told you that, did she?" The old man was being loud and obnoxious.

"She's not daffy!" The woman who saw the cat was taking offense at the words. "I can see the cat too! But I'm a clairvoyant. I see and feel things others don't."

"Oh my, here she goes! Will you quit with your insane spook stuff!" The man seemed to know the woman well, and did not mind insulting her.

A woman in a beautiful scarlet housecoat spoke up, "To lend some sense to all of this, let's go get the scrapbook on the history of Rosehill. It's out in the lobby."

"Are you daft? At this hour?"

"Don't insult me, you big bully! I'm not like your sniveling little wife who is willing to take that from you! You mean nothing to me! It's bad enough I have to put up with you in the library and sitting room, but I'll be darned if I will tolerate you beyond the social rooms! You are a bigot, and an old fool!"

The woman adjusted the belt on her housecoat and stood taller as though to assert herself. The man shook his head and laughed. It was quite amusing watching them spar.

"Look," I cut in, "we'd better wait for daylight when our actions will seem less suspicious. They're watching me already. I'm considered a rebel here for violating the Rosehill rules."

"Brilliant! So what can we get into in your room, Miss?" said the lady in scarlet. "If we go back into the hall, they will hear us going to our rooms."

"You can't stay here all night!"

"Why not?" asked the man.

"I don't want to stay here!" came the whimpering voice of his wife as she flinched from Tabby who was now generously rubbing against her leg.

"All right, here is what we can do. If you will help me fix the bed, the ladies can sleep with me, and you can sleep in one of the chairs!" I said to the man.

"Sounds logical to me!" one of the women said.

"Yes, it makes sense!" said the other.

"Oh, no! There goes my aching back!" the man grumbled. "How did I get myself into a pickle with a bunch of demanding women?"

We worked together pulling the big walnut Victorian bed away from the wall enough to lift the edge of the heavy mattress on both sides. The women weren't much help, and the man complained more than he worked. We all laughed as we fumbled the mattress to the center of the floor.

"Oh, look there, the center slat has dropped down!" said the man.

"I see that, and we just need to replace it on the rail and put the mattress back," I suggested. I pulled the heavy slat from the floorboards and replaced it. "Ready, set, heave!" I yelled as we all grabbed the mattress and dropped it clumsily on the bed slats. It made a booming thud, but the slats held.

"Hooray!" shouted the man. "Now let's get some sleep!" Just then the regulator clock chimed eleven times, and the ladies were as anxious as I was for some rest. They climbed in, and Tabby climbed in with them. I helped the gentleman with extra bedding for his chair.

"Are you sure I must sleep here tonight?" he begged.

"I'm certain!" I said, pointing a finger at the blanketed chair. He complied, but I was sure it wasn't the last I'd hear from him about it. He was a curmudgeon who found everything to complain about, and would elicit my guilt before morning.

At 11:30 P.M., the ladies were snoring. Tabby had disappeared, and the man in the chair was slumping forward uncomfortably.

I was wide awake and a reluctant witness to it all. I quietly retrieved *Adam Bede* from the nightstand and opened it to a random page. I began to read.

> Bright, admiring glances from a handsome young gentleman, with white hands, a gold chain, occasional regimentals, and wealth and grandeur immeasurable. Those were the warm rays that set Hetty's heart vibrating.

It was the experience I'd had earlier as I lay on the bed. The passage was about Hetty, the dark-haired butter maid, and the handsome young man who longed to spend time with her. It was all in the book! Chills went up my spine, and the hair stood up on the back of my neck. I let out a loud sigh, waking the clairvoyant.

"Everything all right, Miss?"

"Yes, go back to sleep. I'm fine." I spoke rudely to the clairvoyant, and felt the need to apologize.

"I'm sorry, I said, "this place, this book, the experiences—all of it has me a bit freaked out. I can hardly cope with Miss Brook every day. I shouldn't be saying these things, but I'm beside myself! All of this seems like a bad dream—no, a nightmare—something from my childhood. I'm sure you don't want to hear me whining, especially at this hour. And yet, you may be the only one who can understand me because you can see and feel things others cannot. There's something very strange about this place!"

"I know what you mean," she said. "Max and I feel the same in our room, and I see so much in this room too. I can't wait until our experience is over! It is hard enough being a clairvoyant in my own surroundings, but Max insisted that Rosehill would make a nice getaway for our anniversary."

"Wait, you mean you see more than Tabby?"

"Oh yes, Miss. I see a woman going through clothing in your wardrobe. There's a short man in black wearing a top hat and tails. His hair is mussed—maybe wet."

"It's greasy!" I said.

"Can you see him too?"

"I saw him in the library twice."

"Are you a clairvoyant?" the woman asked.

"Not to my knowledge. But I believe I did see the woman you mentioned. She was reading in the library. She appears real to me; not ghostlike."

"If you saw her, you'd never forget her, Miss Beck."

"What do you mean? What makes her stand out to you?"

"Her teeth! They are large and crooked, and her chin is long. Her head is too large for her body."

"It's Marian!"

"She is looking at me. She says her name is George Eliot."

"Wait! Marian has a pseudonym. She reads the novels by George Eliot in the library. There's a connection."

"She is pointing to the book in your hands. Did she write that book, Miss?"

"It would seem so. I wonder why she appears real to me and ghostlike to you?"

"Miss Eliot must know you need to see her as real, and after all, this is your experience, not mine. We have our own experience to cope with in Room #3, the Steinbeck Room. At least you aren't dealing with a drought, a dust storm, migrant workers, starvation! I could go on."

I lay the book on the nightstand and pulled the covers up over my head. "No more," I said. "Goodnight!"

I regretted that I was so intolerant of the spiritual. I was not raised to understand such things—had never had to confront the ethereal. The cat had been enough to challenge my thoughts about reality, let alone two dead people poking around my room—living in an alternate dimension, stepping into mine just long enough to make me question my sanity.

"Goodnight, Miss Beck." The clock chimed twelve times, rhythmically like the pounding of my own heart.

"All is well now. They're gone. And so is the cat."

I breathed the stale air under the blankets until I could no longer stand it. I yanked the covers off just in time to see the old man tumble from the chair to the floor and continue his rest without missing a beat. He began to snore. The women slept through it as though they had been seasoned to guttural sounds, or perhaps their own snoring prevented them from hearing his chainsaw eruptions.

How I longed to be taken up into Hetty's world once again. My mind, my body, my heart needed escape. I knew I might be playing with fire, but if I were to fall asleep and dream, what harm would that do? But then again, I was sharing a bed with two women, and the snoring man on the floor could put a dent in anyone's dream life.

What a story I had to tell Mr. Cooper when I saw him again: the ghost cat, one hundred ninety three year old George Eliot accompanied by her mate whose name is also George, a late night room party of elderly people— one a clairvoyant who sees and hears ghosts, and my Hetty dreams that seemed to leap from the pages of a book. He would never believe it—never!

Revelation

Chapter 14

Thunder clapped. Lightning lit up the back pasture like so many fireworks were ringing in Chinese New Year. Another storm! I rose from the crowded bed, and walked to the west window. Pulling the drapes aside, I could make out human shapes in the back pasture. Was I still dreaming? I wanted to dream, but about Arthur Donnithorne and Hetty, not creepers running around the back pasture during a thunderstorm at night. I waited at the window for another lightning strike to reveal more clues.

I began to shiver. I needed a grown-up talk with Mr. Cooper to get through this. If only my phone were working. What were they doing out there on a night like this? All sorts of creepy thoughts shot through my head. What if someone died at Rosehill and….NO! I refused to think such thoughts. After all, I was a journalist with my feet planted firmly in reality. I would go out to see for myself.

The elderly ladies were awake now and stretching. I could see their shapes as they rolled out of bed.

"What time is it, Miss?" We'd better go to our rooms now before they start serving breakfast."

"Brilliant idea!" I said.

"Max, get up, and get your sorry self moving. We mustn't be discovered in Miss Beck's room!" The lady in Scarlet was the deciding factor when she stepped on the old man as he lay sprawled on the floor in front of the bed. He let out a disrupted snore and groan.

"I'm up!" he said, dragging his blankets with him into the chair. "What time is it?"

"It is time for you to stop asking questions and get up!" his wife urged.

Just then the chimes on the regulator clock sounded six times. I never saw elderly people move so quickly! Out of the door they tiptoed, and across the hall to their own rooms. I saw the couple go to Room #3, but the lady in scarlet kept walking until she disappeared in the darkness of the hall. I imagined her as a guest in the Hawthorne Room #7. Or perhaps she was another ghost of the house. But surely the clairvoyant would have said so; she could see ghosts.

The rain had stopped, the room was still, and I felt sleepy. I fluffed the blankets and climbed back into bed. It was a restless sleep with images fading in and out—a field, two farmhands working hay ricks. A horse carrying a uniformed gentleman galloped by. It reared in front of me as though to reveal the rider. It was Arthur Donnithorne, Eliot's young captain who woos the seventeen year old butter maid, Hetty. The lucid dream went on for what seemed an hour, but it had only been fifteen minutes by the regulator chime. It amounted to a power nap.

I wanted to lie on the bed and remember everything I'd dreamed—to languish in the images of Arthur on the white steed. I tried.

"Miss Beck, your breakfast tray is served."

"Just place it on the hall stand, Miss Matthews. I will be out to retrieve it shortly."

"Whatever you say, ma'am." I heard the maid clear her throat, but she said nothing more. Her footsteps continued down the hall. What did she want to say to me?

"Miss Beck!" I knew that shrill voice anywhere.

"Yes, Miss Brook?"

"I would like to speak to you after breakfast."

"Of course. How about 10:00 A.M. in the lobby?"

"Fine!" She snorted and stomped away.

There was another knock at the door and a testing of the knob! "Who is it?" Yanking open the door, I saw no one—nada—nothing! My knees were shaking. What if it were Marian aka George Eliot, and that little puppet master, Lewes? They requested my company on a trip to England. I must find some way to get out of that obligation for my sanity's sake. I would be talking to ghosts for God knows how long. The cab driver and the flight attendants would think I'd lost my mind. And that would just be the first leg of our journey.

I opened the door a crack to see if the hall was clear. Adjusting my eyes, I saw the silver breakfast tray in the dim gas lamp light. I stepped out to retrieve it. Toast and tea again, and a note from someone! Another note? But wait—this one was not in Marian's handwriting. I set the tray down to open the crimson wax seal on the envelope. It was from George Lewes!

"My dear Miss Beck, Marian and I request the honor of your company in the library this afternoon while the other guests are having punch in the sitting room. Do not reply. We will see you at 3:00 P.M. Yours in sincere friendship, George Lewes and Marian Evans."

Odd! Ghosts can pen and seal invitations? Why would they invite me to the library at 3:00 P.M. when it was forbidden at that hour? I thought to flee the B & B immediately following breakfast, but the sleuth in me had my curiosity piqued. I would go to the library. I would face Marian and Lewes—give them a chance to explain before I ran off with my bag of insecurities and superstitions.

My thoughts began to sound like those of my mother warning me about every crack in the sidewalk, every boy that entered the neighborhood, every skateboard or bicycle. She had such high hopes for me. The twins were a satisfying finish to her maternal efforts. They are there for her and Dad. I was their disappointment—the one that got away—carrying my pen and pad everywhere I went, hoping for the big, bigger, biggest story that would get me to the *New York Times*. But was that what I really wanted?

There was something about Marian that screamed my own life story. She did exactly what she wanted to do when she wanted to do it. I liked that. And her writing took her places she would not have known otherwise. But she was the famous novelist. That was a sure passport to freedom. Or was it?

I dressed and walked down the hall toward the lobby to meet Miss Brook. I lingered at Room #3, the Steinbeck Room. Are they reading *Of Mice and Men*?

Miss Brook was seated at the end of the hall with a basket of party favors in her lap. She didn't look up. She kept arranging ribbons and lace as I sat in the chair next to her.

"Miss Beck, I asked you here to discuss your alarming behavior last evening. We, at Rosehill, run a respectable establishment. We expect the behavior of our guests to parallel the fine service we offer them."

"Miss Brook, you misunderstood the situation. My bed broke, and I screamed out because I was shocked."

"No details, please, Miss Beck! Now, I am giving you one more chance to right your behavior, and then I'm afraid we will have to let you walk without a refund. We regret giving you such an ultimatum, but we sincerely hope you will have a smooth, satisfying experience until your check-out on Friday morning." Miss Brook sounded as though she were describing a wine tasting experience instead of a stay at this second rate B & B out in the middle of sheep country. And who was the "we" she was speaking for?

"I understand completely, Miss Brook. I intend to abide by house rules from now on." What I didn't tell her was that I was invited to the library at 3:00 P.M. by two ghosts—and without house permission!

"You are excused."

"Oh, thank you, Miss Brook. But one more thing, who was in the back pasture this morning? During the thunderstorm—say around 6:00 A.M.?"

"Storm? Lightning? People in a pasture? Oh my...." She walked away leaving me to feel like a fool on one of those silly sitcoms I avoided like a plague.

"Psst! Over here!" I looked around to see Miss Matthews hiding behind the staircase near the kitchen.

"Ma'am, you must try to understand and appease Miss Brook."

"Why?"

"She is old and feeble. She had her hearing aids out during the night. She didn't hear the thunder—slept right through it."

"I see. Poor old girl. It was a bit wicked of me to ask about the suspicious activity in the back pasture, wasn't it? Do you know anything about that, Miss Matthews?"

"No ma'am. I did hear the thunder, and see the lightning, but I was in the kitchen peeling the potatoes for cottage fries at 6:00 A.M. when the storm began."

"Cottage fries sound good right now. I was served only tea and toast again this morning."

"Wait here, ma'am, I'll bring you some leftovers from breakfast." Miss Matthews disappeared behind the swinging kitchen doors, and reappeared holding a bowl of cottage fries and a slice of back bacon. "Sorry it isn't more, but I can't risk Miss Brook finding me at the stove frying up eggs at this hour."

"Thank you, Miss Matthews."

I returned to my room, locked the door, and ate from the bowl like a hillbilly. At that moment I did not care if George Eliot and George Lewes were watching me. I would not have cared if my mother were standing there scolding me. I was famished!

The Master Plan

Chapter 15

After my hearty breakfast, I rested in my bed, tucking in with *Adam Bede*. I hoped to have another dream, or remembrance, or whatever that was. I wanted to know the people in the story—I wanted to know how the simple farm girl, Hetty, sold her soul for the handsome captain. Were they in love? I would bet on it.

After several hours of reading, I learned that Hetty had chosen someone who loved her, but who could not make a commitment because of her class and his rank. I wept for Hetty when I read that she was pregnant by the handsome Captain Donnithorne. He went back to his regiment before Hetty had a chance to talk to him about her pregnancy. In the meantime, Adam Bede, a carpenter and land manager, asked for Hetty's hand in marriage. He had always loved her, but she had shown no mutual interest. Now she needed him more than he wanted her. She wept in his arms as he set their wedding date.

Fearing social disgrace, she did not tell anyone—not even Adam—that she was carrying Donnithorne's child. Hetty had second thoughts about marrying Adam, and set out to find her lover. For weeks, she traveled, stopping only long enough to work for her carriage and lodging along the way.

My heart was breaking for Hetty and Adam too. I was angry with Arthur for having violated Hetty knowing there was no future for them because of the difference in their stations in society. I knew after reading several chapters that I no longer wanted to dream about Hetty and Arthur. My own unrequited love wound was too fresh.

It was half past 1:00 P.M. when I drew a bath in the copper tub. I pulled the fern-patterned curtains across the doorway separating the sleeping area and bathroom just in case George Lewes' ghost was watching! The scent of lavender bath soap filled my senses. I rested my head on the rolled towel at the back of the tub, and thought how fortunate I was to be there, how nice it was of Mr. Cooper and the staff to arrange the stay, and how I'd misjudged Miss Brook for being a snippy, overly-judgmental prude. I was right where I needed to be—in this experience—in this time—in this place.

Wrapping myself in an Egyptian cotton robe, I stepped out into the bedroom area. I was immediately greeted by Tabby. It suddenly occurred to me that Tabby may only make herself known when other ghostly visitors are in the room. But I could see her; so why could I not see George Eliot and George Lewes in my room?

The greater mystery was the fact that everyone else saw the ghosts of Marian and George in the library and sitting room, but only the clairvoyant could see them in my room. And yet, Marian visited me here for breakfast. She acted like a living being, not a ghost. This story was taking on new dimensions daily.

I slipped on a plain black housedress with a button-up front and softly folding train at the back. It nipped in at the waist. I tried the black button-up boots and found them quite comfortable. I slipped my pocket-sized journal into my boot along with a stenographer's pen to take notes as I could.

At 2:45 P.M., I headed for the library, checking both ways as I left my room. I locked the door behind me. I wanted no one in my room—no one living that is.

I padded down the hallway, turned the corner to the sitting room, and continued down the hall to the library. The doors were locked. The lights were out. I felt like a fool standing there testing the knob at that hour. Miss Brook made it clear that it was only open at 8:00 P.M. Where were George and George?

The knob turned from the other side of the door. I pulled my hand back quickly as though I'd been shocked. "Come in, my dear Sara," came the voice of Mr. Lewes. I was looking at the ghost of Marian's husband, and I was expected to respond! Marian was seated at the lounge in the center of the room. She looked up and smiled warmly at me.

"How are you today, Marian? And you, Mr. Lewes?"

"We are very well, my dear." Marian motioned for me to be seated next to her, while George threw his hands behind his back, crossing them. He headed toward the back wall of books. He was clearly a man on a mission. "So tell me, dear Sara. Have you worked out your arrangements for our trip to England?"

"Not yet, Marian. I need to use a telephone to call my boss."

"Didn't you say your Mr. Cooper wanted you to leave Friday on a fact-finding mission to England?"

"Oh, yes, but I do need to find someone to look after my apartment and Cat."

"I see. There are no telephones here, Sara."

"None? I must contact Mr. Cooper!"

"Can someone from Rosehill contact him for you?"

"I should try the maid. She seems agreeable."

"Miss Matthews is a dear person. I've noticed that she is considerate of each guest's needs, and she tries to make amends for Miss Brook's ill-mannered outbursts." Marian searched my face for a response.

"I will ask Miss Matthews today."

"Look there, my dear, it's Miss Matthews in the hall now. Catch her, and then do return to us."

How odd that Marian saw Miss Matthews that very moment as if she had summoned her. I ran to the library doors, pulling them open quickly, and yelling down the hallway at the maid. "Miss Matthews, please wait! I must ask another favor of you."

"Miss Beck, whatever are you doing in the library? You know how Miss Brook will react to your being here!"

"I know, but I had to take the risk. Someone invited me here for a meeting at 3:00 P.M."

"Meeting? What meeting, ma'am? And who is meeting with you?"

"Marian Evans and Mr. Lewes are waiting for me to return to them. I must hurry."

"Hurry? Hurry for what?"

"I need a phone, or someone who has access to a phone. Can you help me?"

"We don't have a phone here, ma'am."

"Yes, I know. I'm looking for someone who lives off the premises who might be able to get a message to my boss at *The Times Herald*."

"We get deliveries on Tuesday. Can you wait until then, Miss Beck?"

"No, Miss Matthews, I must get a message out today."

"Let me see what I can do. Can you write down what you want to say, and maybe I can get the paper boy to drop it in the mail?"

"Here's fifty dollars, Miss Matthews, ask him to get it to the newspaper office today." I pulled my pen and pad from my boot and began to write.

"Miss Matthews! Where are you?" came the familiar, harping voice of Miss Brook from around the corner. "I need you in the kitchen—NOW!"

I jammed the note and money into Miss Matthews' apron pocket and scrambled back into the library. I was not sure I could trust Miss Matthews, but I had no one else to ask. Marian and Mr. Lewes were watching me intently as I approached them.

"All settled then?" Marian inquired.

"I've sent a note to my boss. He should have it today."

"I do hope so, Sara. George and I are determined to have your traveling company."

"I have a ticket for England, but I have no clothes to wear beyond these walls. Everything in my room is from the Victorian period. The clothes I wore to Rosehill have disappeared."

"Look in Room #8, Sara." George said mysteriously.

"Room #8? Why? I'm having enough trouble in my own Room #1. Why would I want to add another dimension of trouble to my current list of woes?"

"Room #8 is the Stephen King Room. Its current occupant is in the sitting room right now, and you can pinch some clothes from his wardrobe. I know you like wearing trousers." Mr. Lewes chuckled at my expense. He knew me inside and out. "He's your size, but he is a bit taller. We can find a tailor in London to take up the trousers for you. Wear an overcoat, and no one will notice the baggy shirt. When we are in London, we will get you fitted with a seamstress who will design lovely dresses for you. Won't we, Marian?"

"Don't take the modern clothes into your room, Sara. Pack a bag, and leave it in the shrubbery that surrounds the front door. The gardener will not be here until next week. It will be safe there," Marian added.

"Go now, and be quick about it. If you are caught, our traveling experience is all over." They ushered me toward the door.

I sneaked out of the library. At the corner, I checked the sitting room door. Inside a light was on, and I could see figures moving around. I tiptoed past and turned the corner to the lodging hall. Room #8 was the first door on the left. I tested the door knob. Open! I heard a noise in the kitchen hall. Then footsteps toward the lobby. With a quick push, I was into Room #8. Darkness surrounded me, and the smell of men's cologne nearly choked me. I felt for the light switch. My fingers fumbled around on what seemed to be grooved wood paneling. Finally I felt something modern, familiar, a wall plate for the light switch.

Much to my surprise, the room looked like my apartment—modern. There was a queen bed set against the north wall. The bedspread had brown and tan stripes, and the curtains matched. A door separated the bathroom and bedroom. I looked around for the closet.

This gentleman had recently arrived. His blank guest card was still laying on the maple desktop. My eyes scanned the room: a television, a landline phone, and a copy of *The Times Herald*! I picked up the phone. There was a dial tone. Shaking, I dialed the direct number for Mr. Cooper's office at *The Times Herald*.

"Mr. Cooper here!"

"Mr. Cooper, it's Beck!"

"Beck, where are you? Why are you whispering? I tried to call you back, but your phone was dead. Don't they have a landline phone in that antiquated place?"

"I'm at Rosehill. I've discovered a phone in the modern room, #8. I must keep our conversation brief. I need to get to England on Friday. Could you send a car for me and two other guests at 6:00 A.M.?"

"Two other guests? Why 6:00 A.M.?"

"Yes, don't ask! I want to get out of here before daylight. How is Cat doing? Is everything OK in my apartment?"

"Yes, Beck, I've had the staff out there every day."

"Mr. Cooper, I don't want the staff in my apartment; only you, or Sharon, the front desk receptionist, please! She's a friend of mine."

"You have friends? Look, I'm busy. Check in when you get to the airport in England."

Click...Mr. Cooper was gone. I set the receiver back in the cradle, and searched the closet for a pair of slacks and a shirt.

Mr. Lewes was right, the occupant of this room was tall and thin, had a preference for earth tones, and possessed impeccably good taste. I found a leather carry-on in the back of the closet, and shoved the slacks and shirt down into the bottom. With my stash in hand, I opened the door of Room #8 and walked into the lobby nonchalantly.

I was a few feet from the front door when a tall young man turned the corner into the lodging area. It was the man who ran out of the library last night. I dropped into a courtesy chair in the lobby, hid the carry-on bag behind the long skirt of my dress, and waited for him to pass. He paid no attention to me—again. He slid his door key into Room #8 and disappeared inside. Much too close for comfort!

Racing outdoors, I tucked the overnight bag into the third shrub down on the right. The left side entrance was closer to the kitchen, and the bag might be noticed from the kitchen window. I smiled at my cleverness. After all, sneaking around—sniffing for a story—was my line of work.

I slipped back inside and down the hallway to my room. I dropped onto the bed and prayed that my plan would work. I was so thankful to be getting out of Rosehill on Friday—even if it meant leaving with ghosts!

I ate a light dinner in my room. I set the tray onto the hall stand, locked my door, and returned to the library to find Marian and George Lewes at 8:00 P.M. There they were greeting guests. Everyone was dressed in finery, and there I was in a day dress of black with no ornamentation. The excitement of the day caused me to forget the library dress code. I saw Calista near the punch bowl being her charming self. She saw me at the same time. Her eyes scanned me up and down in disapproval.

"Miss Beck—Sara, come with me."

"Where are we going?"

"Into the hallway, dearest." I followed her like a scolded child.

"Wear this shawl over your day dress!" She removed her black and red shawl and handed it to me.

"Thank you, Calista. I don't know how to repay the favor."

"You can repay me by returning my shawl before you leave. I know your history of borrowing." She smiled at me as we turned back into the library. Something about her seemed familiar, maternal.

"There you are! What a lovely shawl, Sara." Marian gushed. "It reminds me of the shawls they wear in Spain." She played with the fringe like a young girl dressing a favorite baby doll.

"Sit, and let's talk before someone else discovers you. Sara, you may be wondering why I chose you to go to England with us."

"It had crossed my mind, Marian. There are so many other guests who dress properly, don't borrow books, have perfect social etiquette, and are probably quite well-traveled."

"Well, you see, Sara, that's just it. I don't want the company of someone who is pretentious and studied. You can't know how dry the conversation is among the elite in England. George and I have a lovely time together because we are alike. Yes, we read and write, and entertain friends, but when we are alone, we have the best companionship two people can know. Some nights we laugh so hard that I nearly wet myself. George is quite witty, and I match him in sarcasm."

I longed to be Marian—to have a relationship like hers with George Lewes. Maybe I would find someone to love in England. And even if I didn't, this couple had changed my thinking about life with their model of devotion for one another.

As the evening wore on, the tall, good-looking young man appeared—the occupant of Room #8. His eyes followed me. Did he suspect I'd been in his room?

I thought it best to go to him quickly, and save his announcement to the rest of the room. I could just hear his accusation, "Someone stole my clothes while I was in the sitting room this afternoon!" It would sound something like that. This time he did not turn away as I approached him.

"Miss Beck." He extended his hand to me.

"Yes, and your name, sir?"

"Mr. Donnithorne." There was a twinkle in his eyes.

"No! You can't be Arthur!"

"You're right; he was my great-great grandfather. My middle name is Arthur. My first name is Jacob. It's nice to make your acquaintance."

"Do you mean that George Eliot really knew an Arthur Donnithorne? He's not just a character in *Adam Bede?*"

"I'm told authors write most of their family and friends into their books. I suppose it is natural to write about what and whom you know best.," he replied.

"I see. Are you an author like Marian? It is so nice to talk to someone from the modern era. Sorry about going into your room. I see you read Stephen King. I've never read Stephen King." I was blathering like Jo in *Little Women*—no regulator on my tongue. What must Mr. Donnithorne think of me?

"Yes, I dabble in writing. Everyone I know is writing a book." He chuckled. "As soon as I saw you in the hall, I knew you had been up to something suspicious. I read mostly Stephen King. I'm rereading *Misery* now. It is rumored that King's books are ghost-written. Do you like the scent in Room #8?" Jacob was blathering too.

"Not really. It's rather strong!"

"I thought so too!" We both laughed.

"My room, #1, smells like cloves. Odd that each room has its own scent."

Marian looked up to see where I was. The clock was about to announce the end of our library time. I said good night to Mr. Donnithorne, and walked to her side.

"Sara, have you made a new acquaintance this evening?"

"Yes, he is a distant relative of Arthur Donnithorne, Marian."

She gasped and took my arm. "Promise me that you will not meet him again, Sara."

"Why?"

Marian raised her eyebrows, and I could see that the lines between her eyes were much more noticeable now. She took a deep breath and leaned in.

"Trust me. He comes from a long line of blackguards. He may compromise you."

It seemed she was living through her books—her characters—and I was among them. Did she think I was her friend, Sara Hennell? Marian leaned back, adjusting her veil as though to hide her negative comments about Jacob.

The Getaway

Chapter 16

At 5:00 A.M. Friday, there was a commotion outside my west window. Lightning split the sky revealing a herd of frightened sheep on the hill scrambling for cover. Farmer Newburne and his farmhands were working the herd with a sheepdog. With each crack of thunder, the sheep scattered more. The men's deep voices interrupted the constant sound of rain pelting against the standing seam roof of Rosehill. The softer sounds of sheep bleating added to the pathos. It was a scene right out of nineteenth century England.

After an hour of excitement, the storm ceased. The weary men, the sheepdog, and about twenty exhausted sheep headed north back to the barn. One farmhand, who was closer to the B & B than the others, stopped at the spot where they'd been digging the night before. He tested the ground with his boot, then walked on. How curious it all seemed.

I slipped into a housecoat and put on the comfortable ivory boots. Testing the door to the hall, I detected no human movement. My briefcase and purse in hand, I slipped out through the hallway into the lobby. I was the only soul awake and moving. The ancient oak floorboards were squeaking every few feet. There was a faint smell of gas from the hall lights. They were barely lit—turned down the night before by Miss Matthews.

This was my chance to look at the Rosehill scrapbook while waiting for Marian and George to meet me. I was shaking as I lifted the tome and began to sift through the pages of pasted articles, photos, and various memorabilia. There was a sepia photo in a frame. It looked like Rosehill, but I couldn't be sure. It was covered with vines and had much more gingerbread. I pulled the photo from the cardboard frame. There at the bottom right hand corner was script handwriting from a fountain pen. It read, ROSEHILL, 1850. I was looking at an early photograph of Rosehill! The front yard was all English gardens, and a long walkway of bricks meandered down the hill to a road. Oak trees populated the lawn, and one in particular looked like the patriarch of the property with its branches spreading over Rosehill like an umbrella. There was a red brick coach house in the rear

There was another sepia picture tucked into the back of the scrapbook. The subject in the picture was a woman dressed in Victorian clothing. She looked somber. Her black dress and boots identified the time period. She had upswept hair and horn-rimmed glasses. She held a stack of books. A small cameo ring graced one of her fingers. Who was it? Had she lived here at Rosehill?

Turning the pages quickly, I found a news article. The picture I had just seen was repeated at the top of the newspaper section. I searched for a caption. There it was, "Lady Sara of Rosehill Celebrates the Publication of Her Third Novel, *High Ground*." Had Lady Sara owned Rosehill, lived here, or what?

My heart was racing. I peered down the hallway to see if anyone was coming. My hands were automatically turning pages, searching for more evidence.

There—another article surfaced. "Lady Sara Reads Her New Novel at the Rosehill Library." Same photo. This must have been her standard publicity photo. I drew it closer in the dim light of the lobby. Sara was wearing a white lace blouse, and a dark floor length skirt. A large cameo was at the high neckline. Her face was small and well-structured. Her chestnut hair was swept up in a bun at the back of her head—nothing fussy, no jewelry except the cameo, no hat. Behind her was a desk with a Victorian inkwell stand and a letter box. How intriguing! Lady Sara lived here, and was probably the owner of Rosehill, and the most likely occupant of the Eliot Room #1.

There was a faint knocking sound on the front door. I jumped from my seat to answer it. It was the cab driver to take me to the airport.

"Wait in the car please—oh and pick up my bag in the shrubs there." The young man looked at me like I was one link short of a proper chain. I watched as he tromped through the bushes to retrieve the bag.

"It's wet, ma'am. How long was it out here?"

"Overnight. It will be fine. Set it in the trunk where it won't drip on the carpet of your cab."

"Whatever you say, ma'am." He headed for his cab.

I couldn't wait much longer. It would be daylight, and George and Marian were nowhere in sight.

Suddenly there was a bumping noise from Room #8. The door opened, and out walked Jacob Donnithorne with his bags.

"Where are you going?" I whispered.

"If my cab ever gets here, I am headed for the airport, Miss Beck. And you? Please tell me you are not going out in that robe and slippers?" He laughed out loud.

"Shh! We don't want to wake the others? And they're not slippers; they're house boots."

"House boots? Hah! I don't give a fig about the others. I'm out of here as soon as the car pulls up." He pulled aside the curtain on the front door. "Oh, there it is. Brilliant!"

"Wait, that's my cab. Mr. Cooper ordered it for me yesterday."

"It is just sitting there, and you are just sitting here. What difference does it make if I take this cab, and you wait for another?"

"I have to go before sun up!" I said desperately.

"I see, and why are you in such a confounded hurry?"

"My plane leaves for England today. It's a long drive to the airport."

"So why are you sitting here looking down the hallway?"

"Must you interrogate me, Mr. Donnithorne?"

"Oh, it's Mr. Donnithorne now, is it? I'll tell you what; if you'll allow me to assist you with your briefcase, I will help you to the cab, and we can share it!"

That sounded like a good idea. I took one last look down the hall and saw no one—no Marian—no George. I handed Jacob my briefcase. He placed it on top of his luggage and tethered it down. Just before exiting the door, he threw the key to Room #8 into a tray near the Rosehill scrapbook. "Look at this, will you. "Rosehill, the only B & B that is suited to your favorite time period. We custom design your stay with a theme from any one of our books in the Rosehill library."

Where do you see that?"

"It's on a pamphlet inside the scrapbook."

"Let me see. Footsteps in the kitchen hall! Run!" I followed on Jacob's heels out the door and into the waiting cab. We were a mile down the road before my breathing regulated. Jacob was as cool as a cucumber, going through his itinerary on his cellphone.

"What an odd, old phone you have, Jacob."

"Well, I just hate to get rid of it. I like the way it has a real keyboard."

"Can you drive any faster, sir?"

"My name is Jim—see the license!" he pointed.

"Jim—OK—whatever."

"Miss Beck, aren't you being a bit disrespectful?" said Jacob.

"I'm used to having my own car."

"So is it beneath you to ride in a cab?"

"Not at all. I just prefer my Buick."

"Oh—a Buick! I see."

"You see what?"

"You drive a boring car, Miss Beck!" Jacob went back to his itinerary. He left me speechless—like no one ever had. Except for Mr. Cooper. My car was not boring; it was affordable, respectable, and safe.

"I'm going to take a nap."

"You're certainly dressed for it!" Jacob laughed. "Perhaps you can borrow some more of my clothes while I'm not looking, Miss Beck."

"Very funny! Well as a matter of fact, I may have to do that since the case I left outside in the shrubs got soaked overnight."

"Why was my leather carry-on bag left outside in the rain?" He was not happy!

"Well, I knew I would be in a hurry this morning."

"And why are you in such a hurry, Miss Beck?"

"It may come to no surprise to you that I find Rosehill a bit creepy."

"Creepy, Miss Beck? I find Rosehill fascinating. My room was well furnished, had all of the amenities I expected, and they even provided a Stephen King novel for my reading pleasure."

"You didn't see my room! No modern amenities. Dark and smelling of cloves. The bed caved in one night, and fellow guests helped me pull the heavy mattress off to replace the slats."

"How can that be; you had the best room in the house?"

"Maybe in the 1850s it was the best room in the house!"

"What do you mean, Miss Beck?"

"I had the George Eliot Room #1, which looked like someone shut the door when Lady Sara died, and never opened it again until the day of my arrival."

"How intriguing! Tell me more, Miss Beck."

"Well, there was this wardrobe, and there were clothes that changed themselves out each day...."

"Are you sure you were not in the C.S. Lewis Room, Miss Beck?"

"You mean *The Lion, the Witch, and the Wardrobe*?"

"Precisely."

"Oh, there is no sense sharing more details. Men!"

"Do you smell cloves, Beck?"

"Very funny! And don't call me Beck. Mr. Cooper calls me Beck. He infuriates me!"

"He seems to care for you."

"What do you mean?"

"You said he called for your cab to the airport."

"Oh, that, yes. He seems to think I need some time away—a break. That's why I'm going to England—that, and Mr. Cooper wants me to look at some timeshares for him."

"Mr. Cooper sounds like a good friend, Miss Beck. We must thank our stars for such interventions in our lives. Now, please take your nap so that I can get some texting done."

Something about the way Jacob talked to me made me feel like a child. No wonder he understood Mr. Cooper. They were carbon copies!

Two's a Crowd!

Chapter 17

The cab bounced along the back road for what seemed to be an hour. Conversation was strained, and Jim, the driver, kept looking back to see if his two passengers were sniping at each other. I'm sure he thought we were married and having a disagreement. I tried to ignore Jacob Donnithorne by taking in the scenery around Worthing, Clinton, and out onto the freeway heading to the airport. I decided I'd better be civil to him so that the entire trip would not be miserable.

"So, you never said which airport you were flying into, or where you were going in England."

Jacob did not look up, but replied almost under his breath as he continued to text. "Birmingham."

"You are flying into Birmingham? That's where I'm going!"

Jacob lifted his head, and looked straight at me. "You don't say?"

"It's true. Look at my ticket."

"My luck." He laughed and went back to texting.

"Where are you going from the airport?" I asked.

"The Midlands."

"Where in the Midlands?"

"Warwickshire."

"Where in Warwickshire?"

"The Griff."

"The Griff? That sounds familiar. Is that a hotel?"

"Partly."

"Partly hotel and what?"

"Beefeater Grill."

"So why are you staying there in—what town is it?"

"Nuneaton."

"No! That's where I'm going!"

Jacob looked up from his phone and stared me square in the eye. "You'll find plenty of places to stay in the Nuneaton area."

"But you have our clothes."

"Our clothes? I tell you what; how about if I give you my overcoat. Then you can ditch the robe, and you won't have to worry about staying at the old house with the likes of me."

"Old house? I thought you said it was a hotel and restaurant?"

"It is all of those. An old author used to live there."

"How old is the house, and who is the author?"

"Look it up on the internet. Griff House."

"My phone battery is dead."

"I suppose you want to use my phone?"

"That would be nice."

Jacob shoved the phone into my lap, and heaved a huge sigh. When we get to the airport, find a charging plug for your phone! And take off that ridiculous robe, and wear my overcoat.

"Thank you!" I looked up Griff House in Nuneaton, England. There was a photo of the red brick manor house. Lovely. There were several paragraphs to read, but eventually I found the author's name. George Eliot also known as Mary Anne Evans and Marian Evans! I gasped and Jacob grabbed his phone.

"Are you looking at my private mail?"

"Heavens no! Why would I do that?"

"You entered my room and took my clothes and leather carry-on; why wouldn't you read my mail?"

"I'm sorry I entered your room, but George Lewes told me I'd find some modern clothes to fit me there. He knew that Room #8 was the Stephen King Room with modern amenities."

"Oh, that makes it OK? Who is George Lewes?"

"The lover of George Eliot."

"Say what?"

"They were soulmates who lived together from 1853 until George Lewes' death in 1878."

"And who is George Eliot?"

"George Eliot was a nineteenth century novelist who wrote some of the best British literature. It says on the website that George Eliot is the female equivalent of Shakespeare. But unlike lofty male writers, George Eliot was a woman. She used a male pen name so that she would be taken seriously in the male-dominated literary circles.

Jacob threw his head back and laughed. "I have never heard of her! Where did they live? What books did she write?"

"She wrote *Middlemarch, Adam Bede, Silas Marner,* and many others. Her real name was Mary Anne Evans, though she went by the name Marian for awhile."

"Did she live in London?"

"She grew up in Warwickshire in a small town by the name of Nuneaton."

Jacob turned his full attention to me now. "I suppose you will tell me next that she lived in the old house called Griff?"

"Ah, yes, that is what I am telling you."

Jacob went to the last web search on his phone. He clicked on the link for the Griff, and sat back in his seat. It was obvious he did not believe me. He read several paragraphs, and let out an exclamation. "Of course! Of course you are going to the Griff House with me! You are going there because you know George Eliot and George Lewes, right?"

"Ah, yeah."

"Great—just great!" He put his phone away and threw his full weight back against the seat.

"I'm sorry."

Suddenly the cab driver communicated from the front to say that we were just moments from the airport. "Which terminal?"

Jacob shouted the information through a small hole in the Plexiglass divider.

"That will be $57.00." Jacob looked at me, holding out his hand for my half of the fare.

"I don't seem to have a credit card with me." I opened my wallet and poked around inside. "I always have a credit card. Where is it?"

"Of course you don't have a credit card!" He paid the driver and thanked him. We climbed out with our carry-on bags and headed inside to the TSA Security area. Jacob was racing ahead of me. "When does your plane leave? Mine is leaving in half an hour. Gate 3, American Airlines."

I looked down at my ticket and saw my departure time. "Dare I tell you?"

"No, you aren't on the same plane?" He stopped to compare tickets. "Well, at least our seats are not together!"

"But they aren't too far apart." I laughed and ran up beside him feeling happy to have company on the trip. Besides, he had the clothes! We made it through the screening area in record time.

"There's the gate. Run! They're already loading passengers." Jacob was in command, and I was a willing follower.

"Tickets and photo IDs please." The lady checked our credentials and allowed us to pass. "Just in time; they are ready for departure."

Jacob ran ahead and took his seat, stuffing his bag in the overhead compartment. My seat was on the other side of the aisle and two rows behind Jacob's.

"See you on the flip side then?"

"What else?" He managed a half smile. He retrieved a book from his jacket pocket and immediately began to read. Of course, he was reading Stephen King.

"I will just go on to my seat now." Jacob was paying no attention. I stuffed my carry-on into the overhead compartment, and dropped into my seat. There was no one at the window seat, so I moved over and fastened my seatbelt. I had one last look at Jacob before I adjusted myself for a long nap. I never heard the roar of the jet engines as we departed.

I awoke to find a flight attendant standing in the aisle asking me if I wanted a drink or something for lunch. "Of course. I would like a salad with Melba toast and tea."

"We don't have Melba toast, but we do have crackers. What kind of tea would you like? We have commercial iced tea in a can."

"Crackers will work," I said. Instead of iced tea, do you have white wine?"

"Yes, we do. Chardonnay all right?"

"Yes. And do you have any chocolates?"

"Chocolates?"

"You know—candy?"

"I'm sorry, no candy. We do have chocolate biscuit cookies." She searched her cart to fill my order, handed me a tray, and half a glass of Chardonnay.

"Thank you. I may want a second glass of wine."

"I'll check back with you. Enjoy." The flight attendant walked one seat back where a demanding passenger gave her a hard time about the lunch menu choices.

I tipped the glass to my lips and took a few sips. I looked to where Jacob was sitting on the other side of the aisle. He was sipping wine too. Still reading his book!

"Are you ready for your second glass of wine?" the flight attendant asked.

"Yes, please."

She poured another half glass full of the Chardonnay, and set it on my tray. "That will be $20.00."

"Twenty dollars? Oh—yes, for the wine you mean."

"I can swipe your credit card here."

"I don't have a credit card with me."

"Do you have cash?" the flight attendant said, looking down her nose at me.

"No, but actually, that man two rows up on the right is paying for my flight necessities." I pointed at Jacob. The flight attendant furrowed her brow, and walked to Jacob to ask for payment. Jacob shot me a look that could only be called indignant. He reached into his wallet, and paid my bill.

"No more wine for you!" he yelled. He stuck his head back into his book. The passengers behind him looked at me as though I had a drinking problem. I shrugged my shoulders. How could I tell them that I didn't have my credit card or cash with me? I had never felt so dependent—well not since leaving my family back in farming country.

The wine made me sleepy, but I needed to use the restroom. My bladder would not wait. I stood up, reeled a bit, and started back to the restroom. I stumbled into the closet-like stall. The next thing I knew, someone was banging on the door. I'd fallen asleep on the commode. I hurriedly collected my senses and stepped out only to find it was Jacob who had been pounding.

"What were you doing in there? Sleeping?"

"As a matter of fact, I was!" I teetered stepping into the aisle. Jacob took my arm and walked me to his seat row and sat me down in the empty window seat.

"Sleep it off!" He walked back to retrieve my briefcase and purse. That's the last thing I remember until he woke me for dinner. "More wine?" he asked. It was clear he wanted me to sleep.

Birmingham or Bust

Chapter 18

The late morning sky over Birmingham airport was sunny. I stretched to wake myself. Jacob was already bumping around in his seat, gathering and collecting his belongings and stuffing them into his bag. He was managing my bags too. He seemed oddly paternal—out of character at that moment. Perhaps he felt guilty for pushing the additional wine on me. I was pleased to have it so that I could sleep the long distance over the pond. I hoped I didn't snore or drool.

"We're here," Jacob said. "Quickly, take your carry-on. You'll have to brighten up, Beck!"

"Beck? What happened to Miss Beck?"

"That was over when I paid for your first round of wine!" He smirked, and then tilted his head to make sure I understood."

"OK, Donnithorne!"

"Shh! I don't want folks to know who I am here."

"What's that? You have a reputation here?"

"You might say that, but don't try to use it against me. You may get quite a surprise."

"I wouldn't do that to you, Jacob. But please don't call me Beck. Only the obnoxious Mr. Cooper calls me Beck."

"Perhaps it is a term of endearment for him. He sounds like a generous chap to me. OK, no more Beck. Take this bag, and keep up." Jacob stepped out into the aisle and moved forward in the plane. He looked back now and then to make sure I was still behind him.

"I'm here. I don't need a nursemaid."

"There you go again, Miss Beck! You think you are so independent, but you are not!"

"What?"

"Why do you keep asking WHAT?"

"Just like Mr. Cooper."

"Come on. Move a little faster so we can get a cab out to the Griff and get some lunch. You must be starved by now."

We walked through the commercial area of the airport. Jacob said it was small compared to Heathrow, but friendly. He liked that. We passed a restaurant, a combination gift shop, news stand, and a coffee bar. Once outside, we saw a row of cabs. Jacob stepped to the curb and waved one down.

"Where to?" asked a driver in a red turban.

"Griff House, Nuneaton."

"Let me get your bags for you." He loaded our carry-ons and my briefcase into the back, and started the meter. Soon we were bumping along a beautiful back road.

"Could this be Stratford, Jacob."

"Not even close, Miss Beck. Stratford is well south of here. Maybe you can go on an excursion while you're in England. You could enjoy a play at the Royal Shakespeare Theatre, walk along the Avon River, visit the amazing bakery shops in Stratford."

"That sounds lovely. I guess you've been there?"

"Indeed I have. It is one of the most delightful places in England."

"What brought you to England before this, Jacob?"

"Business. My father owns timeshares in England, and an estate in the Midlands. I fly here to manage things quarterly."

"Oh to have a job like that!"

"No one who is married would have a job like mine."

"I have never been married, Jacob. I'm set in my ways. I would make a terrible wife."

"Indeed!" Jacob almost snorted saying it. He was very pleased with himself.

"You?"

"Me what?"

"Are you married?"

"Heavens no! I'm too set in my ways."

"Well, I guess we are safe traveling together."

"Was there any question?" He broke into a full belly laugh. "If you could have seen yourself drooling on my shoulder. And you snore, Miss Beck!" My worst fears had been realized. I'd made a total fool of myself.

"Well, had you been sleeping, I'm sure I would have heard you snoring. And, in fact, you are almost salivating with sarcasm. I see how you are!" I crossed my arms and went silent. I was more humiliated than angry.

Jacob was quiet too. He sat back and watched the driver as he made his way through the countryside. It was spring in the Midlands, but the hills were steeped in grays and browns, quite unlike the springs in the Midwest U.S. Back home, the daffodils, jonquils, and tulips forced up before spring, and by Easter the flowers were decorating the lawns and sidewalks just in time for festive egg hunts. It mattered—the weather, the flowers, the festivities.

"We are nearing Griff."

"Thank you, sir." Jacob leaned forward to check the meter and took out his credit card to pay. The driver parked at the side entrance of the hotel. It didn't appear to be anything special. The driver set our bags out, and shook our hands. Before he pulled away, he was on the radio for his next fare.

"How efficient he is, and how pleasant." I knew that somehow reflected on me. I did not acknowledge the remark. I picked up my bags and walked straight to the Griff front desk.

"I need to use your phone please. This will be an international call. You may bill it to my room."

"May I see your credit card, ma'am." The clerk was very businesslike. Jacob stepped up to the desk and dropped his card on the counter.

"How did you expect to pay for the room, or the call?" He was rubbing it in.

"I will pay you back. I need to call Mr. Cooper to get money wired."

"You mean you will ask that intolerable old man to wire you money?"

"Very funny, Jacob."

"It wasn't meant to be funny. Just being realistic."

I picked up the desk phone and made a long distance call to the U.S. "*The Times Herald*, may I help you?"

"Sharon! How are you? I miss you. We should get together when I get back from England."

"I'd love that, Sara. Give me a ring when you get home. We'll take in a movie, go shopping, get some pizza. Did you want to speak to Mr. Cooper?

"Yes, please. Going out with a good friend sounds so inviting. You have no clue who I have to put up with here!"

"Hang in there! Hold on for Mr. Cooper, Sara." Sharon was more like a sister than a friend. She was quiet, and liked her privacy too, so a low-key friendship between us worked. What Mr. Cooper lacked, Sharon more than made up for at the front desk of *The Times Herald*.

I was connected to Mr. Cooper's office. I could hear his chair springs squeaking all the way across the Atlantic Ocean.

"Beck? Where are you?"

"I'm in England—Nuneaton—at the Griff House, Premier Inns Hotel."

"What to hell are you doing there?"

"It's a long story, Mr. Cooper. I need you to wire me some money. I lost my credit card."

"How much? And how did you know that I needed you to drive into that area?"

"I need a few thousand, Mr. Cooper. I don't know how long I will be here."

"I'll get Sharon on it right away. What's the address of the nearest bank?"

"I'm not sure. Hold on." I asked the clerk. "Here is the address, Mr. Cooper. It's a bank in Coventry."

"Got it, Beck. The money should be there by noon tomorrow. How was your flight? Make any friends?" He laughed.

"Not you too, Mr. Cooper!"

"What do you mean by that, Beck?"

"Well, it's a long story. When I get to my room and have my phone charged, I will call you and fill you in."

"You sniffed a story! I can tell."

"Later then, Mr. Cooper. Thanks for your help."

"Sure." There was a click at the other end. I hung up the hotel desk phone, suddenly feeling very alone.

"Here is your room key, Miss Beck." The clerk leaned forward over the counter, and took a good look at me. I must have looked comical wearing a man's overcoat, not to mention the ivory house boots.

"Where is your room, Miss Beck?"

I looked at the key. "Room #102."

"It's at this end of the hall, just up these stairs." Jacob walked ahead holding doors. "There it is." He took my key and opened the door for me. I snapped on the light and set my bags down. I turned to thank Jacob, but he was already gone. Here I was in this big hotel across the Atlantic Ocean with no money for food. It would be a long night.

I retrieved the clothes from the wet carry-on, and hung them over the shower rail. I took a long soak, and dressed in a hotel robe. No sooner did I snap on the television, there was a knock at the door.

"Miss Beck, it's me Jacob. Would you like to go downstairs for lunch with me?" I was stunned. I thought I'd heard my last from Jacob.

"Sure, if you would like company."

"If you'll open the door, I will give you a change of clothes from my case." I began to weep. I'm not sure why.

"Thank you, Jacob. The other clothes I borrowed are still damp. What time should I meet you for lunch?"

"1:00 P.M.?"

"I'll be ready." I closed the door, and nearly jumped to the ceiling. Jacob wanted my company.

Promptly at 1:00 P.M., Jacob knocked on my door. He walked me down the hotel back stairs into a lovely restaurant, and through a series of doors that led to a long wrap around bar.

"You certainly look better dressed, even if those are my clothes you are wearing. Would you like a beer?"

"No thank you. I had enough alcohol on the plane!"

"A burger and fries then?"

"I never eat greasy burgers and fries. But suddenly that sounds incredible."

"Waiter, is Chef Dave here?" The waiter nodded. Then we'll have two deluxe onion ring steak burgers with a large side of fries. I'll have a pint, and what would you like, Miss Beck?"

"Oh, maybe a hot cup of tea with honey."

"Not sure we have honey, ma'am."

"Whatever you have is fine." I sat back against the oak booth in the room adjacent to the bar.

"Dave, a friend of mine, is the lunch chef at Beefeater. He specializes in American fare. It's popular in England."

The lunch company could certainly be worse. I smiled at Jacob, and he smiled back. Against all odds, we were becoming friends.

The Ghosts of Griff
Dream

Chapter 19

I was restless all night in my room at Griff. I dreamed of Marian and her soulmate, George Lewes. They were in London in a narrow three-story building. Marian, the person, aka George Eliot the author, was pacing the floor. Her new novel was in the works. She was trying to think of a title for the book. She tested several ideas on Lewes.

"Sister Maggie? No, The House of Tulliver?"

"Marian, let publisher Blackwood chime in with his thoughts on the title. After all, he does this for a living."

"Brilliant, George. I do wish I could take you back to Griff House. I miss its homely presence: the fireplace snug near Father's old office, the polished stone floors, the dark furniture, the cluster of outbuildings that shelters dairy cows and two dozen chickens. There is a delicate dovecote with tiny dome windows—that is perhaps my favorite place outdoors. I used to sit and watch the doves as they came and went through the tiny windows. It was my job to feed them, and make sure they were safe on their roost come nightfall. They would fall prey to the barn owl if not tended regularly.

The driveway snakes in from Gypsy Lane and winds in a circle at the front door of Griff. In the center of the circle is a small yew tree and a water well nearby. Someday, George, I may go back to Griff. Isaac prevents me now, but one day, Isaac may not be there."

"Wish poor Isaac well. He is tethered by his beliefs, Marian. One day he will appreciate you for who you really are—a bright, capable woman who just happens to be one of England's best-selling authors. He will outgrow the pettiness and forgive you. You will see." He stepped closer to her and hugged her from behind.

"Oh, I do hope you are right, George. I trust your instincts on such things."

"I especially appreciate your new novel because it is about you and your life at Griff. It personalizes you. The public comes to know you and empathize with you through the young girl, Maggie Tulliver. Pathos—it's all about the pathos, Marian."

"I got lost in this novel, George. I felt I was there as I was writing. In my mind, I could see the attic where I used to play and read. I saw the fishing hole where my brother and I used to play. I could almost smell the mincemeat pies Chrissy and I made in the brick oven."

"You paint with words, Marian, and your readers will surely observe and appreciate the landscapes of your autobiographical novel."

"I do believe it is my favorite piece of writing thus far, George. It came from the depths of my being."

"Let's go to bed now, Marian. Tomorrow John Cross is coming for a visit. We have some financial business, and then I will have Rufa serve scones and tea. Will you read to him a chapter or two of your new as-yet-untitled masterpiece?"

"Of course, but only if John is agreeable. You are warmth in every way, George. It is no wonder we have so many friends."

They walked through the sitting room arm-in-arm and into their dark bedroom. George lit a lamp for Marian so that she could remove her house booties and climb into bed. "Would you like me to read, Marian."

"Not tonight, George."

Déjà Vu

Chapter 20

I peered out of the fogged window at the end of the hall. A cat was walking on a lower level roof. Above were small windows in what appeared to be a third story attic. I was trying to decide where the hotel ended and the old Griff house began. The cat seemed preoccupied with something it had spotted, and did not notice me watching it through the hotel window.

"Good morning, ma'am!" A maid was approaching me from the other end of the hall near my room. Did you rest well?"

"Indeed I did. Thank you. There is a cat stuck on the roof." I pointed to the Tabby sitting near the gutter.

"Oh, no ma'am, that is Sebastian. He lives in that apartment where you see the windows. Notice that the farthest window is open a bit. They let the cat out for fresh air in the morning, and it climbs back through the window when it is ready."

"Oh, I'm glad to hear that! I was concerned for the cat. He is so close to the edge of the building."

"He has never tried to jump, ma'am. He seems to enjoy it out there. He watches for birds, but the birds are smarter than Sabastian. There's a dovecote near."

"A dovecote, you say?"

"Yes, ma'am, around back."

"I would love to have a look and take some pictures."

"The grounds are open to the public, ma'am, and there's a snug and front office open at the front of the house. Just pass the bar downstairs, and stay toward the front of the house until you see a small room with a snug."

"Snug? What's a snug?"

"You know, a fireplace, ma'am."

"Oh, yes, of course. Thank you. You have been so helpful."

"Have a good day, ma'am."

I said goodbye to the cat, and headed back to my room to collect my camera and notebook. I stopped in my tracks when I realized I had seen the dovecote and the fireplace before. Or did I dream that? My heart was racing. My sense of reality had been challenged for days, so why should it be any different now? I walked downstairs and through the dining room, past the bar and on to the fireplace. I knew then that I had seen it before, the polished brown stone flooring, the small front office that had been used by Mary Anne's father. I shot a round of photos, and took notes on the décor. The small door leading out of the office had several antique bolts and chain locks.

"Miss Beck?"

"You startled me, Jacob!"

"I went to your hotel door, and the maid was cleaning your room. She said you'd come down to take some photographs."

"Yes, I'm headed outdoors now to take some photos and scribble a few notes."

"Sleep well, Miss Beck?"

"Indeed I did, Jacob. That lunch was so delicious. I never knew a hamburger could taste so good. And thank you for sending dinner to my room. They woke me, and I ate like a baby fresh from a nap!"

"You are welcome, Miss Beck. I'm glad to be of help. I caught up with a young lady friend at the bar last night. She's the daughter of the hotel manager. I inquired about your George Eliot, and she said she sleeps in the very attic room that is described in her novel, *The Mill on the Floss.*"

"You don't say? Oh, I would love to see it!"

"She will be joining me tonight for dinner. Perhaps you could come too, Miss Beck? She may share more with you since you are familiar with this author. I was tripping over my tongue asking questions about this lady, Eliot. I felt rather silly because I haven't read any of her books."

"You felt silly, and you just admitted that to me?"

"Well, I'm not totally without humility. I blush when a beautiful lady is in the room too, Miss Beck."

"And did you blush at her?"

"Truth be told, yes. She is lovely, and very bright."

"I see. Well, I wouldn't want to spoil your dinner with her this evening, Jacob. Enjoy."

"Wait! Are you irritated about something? Not that that would be unusual."

"There you go again! You infuriate me, Jacob!"

"Now, Miss Beck, I thought we might get a cab into Coventry today, but if you are going to be this disagreeable, then we'd better part our ways now."

"Coventry? I need to go to the bank in Coventry to pick up my money."

"Then shall we ride together, Miss Beck?" He smiled knowingly. "I'll call a cab."

"I'll go around back and get some photos of the dovecote while the light is right. I'll meet you outside the hotel office where the cab dropped us yesterday."

"Dovecote, you say?"

"Yes, the maid mentioned it to me this morning. But funny, it seems as though I've seen it before. Only one way to be sure; I'll go look. See you later."

"Not so fast! I want to see the dovecote too."

"Really, Jacob? Or do you have an ulterior motive? Perhaps you want to impress your lady friend later this evening with your rapt attention to detail regarding the dovecote?"

"You are so suspicious of everyone and everything, Miss Beck. Why?"

"It's a long story, and I'm sure you don't have time to hear it. Besides, I have pictures to take before we head for Coventry."

"The photos will wait!" Jacob was insistent.

"Fine, follow me, and we will sit outside while I begin to tell you my story."

"Begin? How long is this story?"

"You see! You don't have the time to listen. And I don't have the time to tell my story to someone who is always looking around to find something else to do!"

"Whoa! Where did that come from?"

"From deep within, Jacob!"

"I will just walk outside with you, and we can look at the dovecote together, and then I will go on and do my business. I really don't mean to upset you. Just trying to be a friend."

"Come along then."

Jacob kept his distance, walking with his hands behind his back. I could tell he was trying not to intrude, but it was too late for that consideration. We rounded the corner of the Griff to find a broad and welcoming front view. There was a mature yew tree in the center of the circular drive. I followed the newly black-topped drive around the corner to a wall which separated the house from its smaller outbuildings.

There was the dovecote! I was seeing it with my eyes, but sensing it with my spirit. Suddenly somewhere deep inside I came to life as a little girl scattering feed for the chickens. Then stepping near the dovecote, I looked up at the domed windows where the doves were coming and going. I can only describe my feelings as an epiphany moment. I felt as though I were flying—like I was one of the doves soaring away from the Griff house grounds, surveying what the author George Eliot knew as her childhood home.

"Are you all right?"

Jacob took my arm just in time to catch me. I had been tilting back as I looked up, not realizing I was losing my balance.

"I'm fine. I guess I've been experiencing too much lately. This past week has been difficult for me. It seems I know this place—the Evans who managed it in the 1800s, and this author George Eliot."

"Do you mean like déjà vu?"

"Could be, Jacob. Could be."

"Come inside for now. Let's get a cup of tea with honey. That should make you feel better."

Jacob walked me back into the bar. We sat in the same wood booth where we sat the day before. It was comforting. "I'll order our tea."

"But you don't drink tea, Jacob."

"I do now; I'm with you." I watched Jacob step up to the bar to order a pot of tea. I saw the bartender scratch his head. "Yes, honey! I know you have it."

"Jacob Donnithorne." A voice shattered the quiet of the dark bar and brought me back to reality. It was the manager's daughter no doubt; she was gorgeous. "Jacob, I have to work tonight. I can't have dinner with you, but I can meet you after I'm off duty." Jacob looked disappointed. "I know it has been a long time since we've chatted, but I have no choice. I could call some of our old friends, and you could catch up with them at the bar. I could join you all later."

Jacob disappeared around the corner with her. He returned quickly, carrying tea.

"Sorry about that." he said.

"What?"

"You know what."

"I haven't the slightest idea what you are talking about."

"OK, play naïve then. Sasha is coming back to show us some photos of Griff. She can't join me for dinner."

"Oh, that's too bad."

"Right. I see you mean that sincerely." Jacob poured the steeped tea into our cups and added honey. We drank the amber beverage slowly. "Would you like an appetizer—some pate and Melba toast perhaps?"

"Do you like Melba toast, Jacob?" I cast a doubtful look his way.

"No, but you do."

"How do you know I like Melba toast?"

"I know a lot of things about you, Miss Beck."

"Now you are 007—a spy only pretending to be a friend?"

"There you go again! Stop doubting me. Listen, we need to get to Coventry to do our business. I'll go to the front desk to call a cab. Meet me there. We'll go to the bank first to pick up your money. I'll pay a visit to the real estate office, and do my business while you look around Coventry. How's that?"

"Thank you, Jacob."

"Thank you, Sara."

Coventry Capers

Chapter 21

The cab driver picked us up shortly after noon. The drive to Coventry was short and sweet. Every hillside, each mature tree, the older homes, all stood out as markers of a bygone era. Perhaps when George Eliot was young, she looked at the same landmarks from a carriage on her way to Coventry.

"What brings you to Warwickshire?" the driver asked.

"We have business here." Jacob replied in a guarded way.

"Griff house has a lot of history dating back to the 1800s. Did you know that some of George Eliot's descendants still live around here?"

"How much do you know about George Eliot?"

"Enough to chat it up with my passengers who stay at Griff and have a mind to share."

"Touche´. Well, Miss Beck has read George Eliot's novels. She's planning a story for her newspaper back in the States."

"I am?" Jacob elbowed me signaling me to be quiet.

"See that spot over there with the old oaks?"

We both craned our necks to see where he was pointing. "That is where Rosehill used to be. Are you familiar with Rosehill, Miss Beck? Miss Beck?" The cab driver looked in the rear view mirror to see me wide-eyed and unresponsive. "Is something wrong, Miss Beck?"

"She's fine. Give her a moment."

"I am familiar with Rosehill. I've been there. I stayed there just last week—Rosehill in the U.S. that is." My mind was racing. Déjà vu!

"Come again? Did you say you stayed at Rosehill last week?"

"Yes, it's a B & B in the Midwest U.S. that offers experiences—kind of like time travel using books to initiate the experience. I'd like to tell you that it was a good experience, but I cannot."

"Why, was it a bad experience, ma'am?"

"It's a long story. But I will give you a snippet. Upon arriving at Rosehill B & B, I was checked into the Eliot Room and given a book by George Eliot. Strange things began to happen. I left Friday. I was never so glad to leave any place in my life."

"So did you enjoy George Eliot's book, ma'am?"

"I did. As a matter of fact, I got caught up in it. I was fond of one of the characters. Her writing draws you into each scene as though you are there."

"Do tell, ma'am? Which book was that?"

"*Adam Bede.*"

"Oh, I see. That was Eliot's first novel. Quite popular then and now."

"You read Eliot's novels?" I know my face looked shocked.

"Of course, ma'am. Everyone reads her novels in the Midlands. We're quite proud of her for having come from these parts."

"Forgive me. I didn't mean to imply you don't read. I'm just shocked that George Eliot is so popular. She's a Victorian author."

"Well Shakespeare and Dickens are still popular too, ma'am." He smiled revealing his crooked teeth. So who were you infatuated with, ma'am?"

My cheeks blushed as the driver's eyes were riveted on me in the rear view mirror. "Captain Arthur Donnithorne." I tried to whisper it, but Jacob's eyes were also now riveted on me.

The driver broke the tension by saying that Arthur was not a good person. "Why, he tore poor Hetty's heart wide open with his fancy, cocky ways and dallying. He left her with child, he did."

"So, you have a crush on my ancestor, the illustrious, and deceased, Captain Arthur Donnithorne?"

"Don't be ridiculous! It was a moment of madness. I got over it quickly when…." Both men stared at me. It was one of the most embarrassing moments of my life.

"Yes, ma'am, go on."

"Yes, do go on, Miss Beck," Jacob snickered.

"Well, when I learned what a hopeless jerk Arthur was, I decided not to risk a dalliance even in my imagination—besides Marian told me he was trouble when she saw me talking with you in the library, Jacob."

"So this all happened in your imagination?" asked the driver.

"Is that why you stopped showing interest in me after Marian called you to her side that night in the library?"

"Well, yes, Jacob. I trusted Marian's judgment. After all, she wrote the character and all of his attributes— good and bad."

"You don't mean Marian Evans, ma'am?" The driver was still watching us through the rear view mirror.

"Yes, I do."

"You've seen Marian Evans and talked to her? At Rosehill?" The cab driver looked worried. "Well, I've heard of ghost stories mostly from Griff guests, but this beats all!" He pulled the cab to the curb as we entered a street in Coventry.

"I'm off duty in an hour. Can't pick you up. Sorry." He sped away after Jacob tipped him a few pounds.

"Don't say a word. I will go into the bank to get my money. Then I will walk around Coventry, and meet you back here at the visitor's center at 2:00 P.M."

"Fine, let's get some lunch. There's a nice place over there." He pointed at an upscale restaurant. Then off he went to conduct his own business.

No words can convey what I was feeling just then. Humiliated would be inadequate. Embarrassed doesn't even begin to touch the edges. I would feel better knowing I had money in my pocket. Yes. I would feel less dependent and vulnerable then.

Mr. Cooper was absolutely right about the time the money would be at the bank. I knew little about the value of British pounds, so I would need to be careful what I spent without Jacob there to advise me.

I went into the visitors' information center to get a guide to Coventry sites. The city was known as the "city of spires." Though I wasn't religious, I was drawn to see each holy site. I read in the tourist literature that Holy Trinity was where Miss Evans and her father attended church. I stepped inside the renovated twelfth century structure, marveling at the artistry of the stained glass windows. In the vestibule was an impressive baptismal font, and above and behind it was a stunning glass window at the other end of the nave, depicting the Christ crucified. What an impactful greeting the two elements made.

I walked to the remains of Saint Michael's Cathedral to get the feel of the damage caused by German bombing raids during World War II. It looked like a large rose-colored skeleton looming over Coventry.

Such a rich and inspiring history ignited my imagination. I took photos from every angle, and almost felt the fear of that period when Coventry was in ruins and smoke was rising from the streets. It evoked sadness and courage in me at the same time.

I made my way into the more commercialized streets where there were dress shops, antique stores, a quaint bookstore, and some restaurants. I window-shopped my way through the city, stopping at one store long enough to admire some clothes I knew would look fabulous on me.

The shop owner stepped out onto the sidewalk and began pointing out the bargains in the window. "Do come in. This dress would be irresistible on you! And it will accentuate your eyes and hair."

"The red one? I don't usually wear red." I pointed to the brown one with soft cream trim.

"So you like earth tones. For tonight, my dear, wear red. Trust me on this." She smiled a broad smile full of perfect teeth. "Try—go ahead! You need to get out of those masculine looking clothes!"

I tried on the red dress that had a flounced chiffon skirt, spaghetti strap top, and a little red bolero style jacket that could be worn for cooler evenings.

"Gorgeous!" she said. "You need these heels to go with it. And this clutch purse. Oh, this is a new line of jewelry that is made for this style evening dress."

She coaxed me until I was dressed from head to toe like one of her window mannequins. She angled the floor mirror and walked me back to get a full view.

"Is that me?"

"I told you, Miss. You look fabulous. You will turn every head in the room with this outfit. Spin and watch how the chiffon flounce moves. Men love that!"

"I don't have a man, and I have no intentions of getting one."

"I can see why you wear men's clothing then, Miss. I don't know why you are bitter, but open your heart to yourself, and shine—if just for one night. Give the dress a try." She sold me the whole outfit in under twenty minutes. This was for me, and I could justify the expense.

I met Jacob at the visitor's center. "Where would you like to go for lunch? What's in the bag? Did you get inside the churches?"

"Goodness, take a breath! What's the hurry? We can talk over lunch."

"You choose the restaurant, Miss Beck."

"I saw this lovely eatery around the corner."

"Let's go then." Jacob took my packages and let me lead the way.

"I see you trying to peek into those bags, Jacob!"

"What's the big secret? I just want to see what you purchased with your money. Do you have any left?"

"Of course I do." I wasn't sure how much though.

I opened the restaurant door and allowed Jacob to pass with my packages. He looked like a beast of burden under the bags and boxes.

"I know you are laughing at me, Miss Beck."

"So now you are a mind reader?"

He set the packages on the floor, and like a gentleman pulled out a chair for me. The décor of the restaurant was definitely English pub style. The walls were dingy white with dark oak cross braces. A waiter filled and carried frothy mugs of beer from the bar tap. The foam dripped down the glasses onto the floor.

"Isn't that dangerous?" I asked.

"No, the peanut shells keep you from slipping." I looked down and saw mounds of peanut shells around the tables.

"I can't believe it! Don't they ever clean this place?"

"Lighten up, Miss Beck, you chose this restaurant. Now we'll have to make the best of it."

Jacob picked up a bucket of peanuts from the center of the table, and began to make a mess as he cracked the shells and deposited them on the floor.

"Now I've seen everything!"

"Trust me when I tell you that you have not seen everything, Miss Beck. In fact, you need your horizons widened. I heard that line in the movie *Becoming Jane*. Jane Austen was being tempted by a worldly man who told her that her writing would be more authentic if she got out into the world and got acquainted with how everyone else lives."

"You watch period movies?"

"Yes, Miss Beck. Does that surprise you? I also go to the symphony, go out on an occasional date, vote, and call my folks on holidays. Unlike you, I get along with people."

"That was low. I vote, and go to concerts. I have dated since my senior year in high school—even had serious relationships. I get along with people, but I prefer my privacy so I can think and get my work done."

Jacob stopped his sarcasm long enough to order a mug of beer.

"And what will it be for you, ma'am?"

"A glass of white wine please."

"We have Moscato. Will that do?"

"Yes, that will be fine."

"Have you ever tried red wine, Miss Beck?"

"No."

"Why not?"

"I've always liked white wine. I stick to what I like."

"I see. Sip some of this beer." He slid the mug over to my side of the table.

"If I take a sip, will you leave me alone?"

"Sure, if you insist."

I took a small sip of the beer, getting mostly foam. Jacob pulled the mug up from the table and walked up to the bar with it. "Fill 'er up!" he said. The bartender refilled his glass from the long ivory-handled tap behind the bar. He walked back to the table and proceeded to drink his pint. He said nothing more until the food came, and only then to thank the waiter.

"Are you ignoring me?"

"You made me promise to leave you alone."

"I didn't mean it that way."

"Do you want me to have a conversation with you?"

"Oh for heaven's sake, Jacob. Don't be sore about your date going wrong tonight. I'll go up to my room as soon as we get back to Griff. You will have ample opportunity to charm Miss Congeniality!"

"For your information, she is a colleague, not a date."

"Oh?"

"She works for me."

"For you?"

"Does that surprise you, Miss Beck?"

"Nothing about you surprises me, Jacob."

"Good, I want to keep you on your toes."

"So, if that lady is not your date, and she works for you, then you are free to have dinner with me?"

"Yes, Miss Beck. Dinner with you."

"Please, call me Sara." My mind raced to the red dress and matching heels. I suddenly felt like taking a slow romantic turn around the floor.

Midnight Madness

Chapter 22

Back at Griff, I took a long soak in the hotel's lavender bath salts. Wrapped in the hotel robe, I threw myself onto the comfy bed and dialed Mr. Cooper's home phone. A woman's voice was at the other end.

"Hello?"

"Mrs. Cooper?"

"Speaking."

"This is Miss Beck from *The Times Herald*. Is Mr. Cooper there?"

"Oh, you must be one of the reporters for the paper. Good to hear you. Hold on, and I will get Mr. Cooper for you."

"Beck?"

"Yes, it's me, Mr. Cooper. I got the money wire you sent. Thank you. I took a cab into Coventry. Did some sight-seeing, had lunch, bought a new dress."

"That's nice, Beck. Now when will you get around to checking the timeshare properties?"

"Tomorrow—I promise."

"I guess you still have that fellow hanging around with you? Is he behaving?"

"Yes, Mr. Donnithorne is still hanging around with me. He's been quite helpful. He reminds me of you, Mr. Cooper." Mr. Cooper laughed and cleared his throat.

"Nobody else like me, Beck. Remember that!"

"How could I forget? Goodnight, Mr. Cooper."

"Goodnight, Beck." And with that he was gone. So abrupt, so much like my father, so much like Jacob. How and why did I keep attracting men into my life that irritated me so?

I pulled the *Adam Bede* novel out of my briefcase. I had some time to read before I put on my red dress and dancing shoes. I opened to Chapter 15.

> The vainest woman is never thoroughly conscious of her own beauty till she is loved by the man who sets her own passion vibrating in return.

I read on for an hour or so. I felt the fiery exchange between Arthur and Hetty. Eliot must have experienced this love for Lewes and transferred her feelings into her novel. I felt the words. My own heart was opening.

The evening news came on the television. Dinner— downstairs—7:00 P.M. I ran to the bathroom to pin up my hair, and put on my red dress to surprise Jacob. There was a knock at the door.

"Who is it?"

"Sasha."

"Sasha? Do I know you?"

"Oh, I'm sorry. I'm a colleague of Jacob's. He sent me to your room to give you these photos and the history I have on the Griff." I opened the door and let Sasha into my room.

"You look ravishing, Miss Beck!"

"Thank you. Please do sit down. I thought you might join us after your shift this evening?"

"Well, something's come up, and I thought I'd better just leave these with you. I went to Jacob's room first, but he redirected me here. I hope it isn't any trouble." She handed over the cache of Griff memorabilia.

"Not at all. Thank you, Sasha. I'm sorry you cannot join us tonight. I will look through this material, and make sure you get these treasures back."

"So you and Jacob are traveling together?

"Quite accidentally, Sasha. Jacob tells me you work for him."

"Is that what he told you?"

"I've gotten too personal. So sorry. Goodnight, Sasha, and thank you again."

"Goodnight, Miss Beck."

I jumped up and down like a schoolgirl knowing I'd be alone with Jacob in my new dress—lights low, music playing, Jacob—being sarcastic as always! What was I thinking? This red dress would make no difference in his behavior. I was acting like a silly school girl, desperate for attention. There was another knock at the door.

"Yes, Sasha?"

"It's Jacob, Sara."

"I'll meet you downstairs. I'm dressing."

"Later then…."

I lengthened my lashes, and applied blush to my cheeks. The tear drop earrings the clerk chose for me accentuated the scoop neckline of the dress. I pinned my hair up, allowing a few strands to fall free at my temples. Now for the finishing touch of lipstick and red high heels! Was it too much?

This new look didn't feel like me, but I didn't really know who I was anymore. I felt like a cross between Miss Beck, Hetty, and George Eliot these days. I checked myself a few times in the mirror, twirling in the chiffon dress as I had in the shop. I read in one of the ladies' magazines that you should put cologne on the backs of your knees, behind your ears, on your wrists, and in your cleavage area. That would be great if I had perfume. I was as ready as I'd ever be.

I walked downstairs and back to the corner booth where Jacob and I had eaten lunch. No Jacob. I asked at the bar. They hadn't seen him. I'll wait. Could I have a glass of Chardonnay please?" I nursed the wine for a half hour. Jacob had not come. He left me sitting there alone in my beautiful red dress. Men were not to be trusted.

"Ma'am, someone at the bar said Mr. Donnithorne is in the dining room waiting for his dinner guest." The bartender returned to his duties. I walked around the bar and into the formal dining room. There was Jacob dressed in a sports jacket standing up at the edge of the table looking for me.

"Oh, Jacob! There you are."

"Oh my!"

"Do you like it—the dress, I mean?"

"Don't take this wrong, Miss Beck, but you don't look like you." He pulled out a chair for me. "Forgive me for staring, Sara. I have never seen you look so lovely since that first night in the Rosehill library when you were wearing that draping blue silk dress."

"You noticed me? You were a wallflower the whole time, and when I approached you, you ran into the hall."

"Guilty! I was intimidated by you. I was new on the scene, and you were hobnobbing with the elites."

"This is amusing. I thought you did not care to spend time with me."

"No, not at all, Sara. I am a bit shy. I do all right in the corporate world, but with women—not so much."

"Let's start over, Jacob. Let's pretend we are meeting for the first time tonight—a date." Jacob was visibly nervous. I was feeling it too. We'd been together for days quibbling like siblings, talking like friends, and spending money together like man and wife. My breathing changed when he took my hand and held it in his. I was nervous beyond reason.

"Shall I order wine?"

"Red wine, please, Jacob."

Turning his attention to the waiter, Jacob ordered. "Can you serve a flight of reds? Surprise us. And a tray of hors d'oeuvres please, but only if C. J. Lowery is the chef tonight. I think he's top notch!"

"Sure, Mr. Donnithorne." The waiter walked back to the bar to fill our order.

"I know you will love the deep, rich layers of the reds, Sara. It is fitting that you should be wearing that red dress tonight—red like the wine you are finally willing to try. Life is about taking chances, trying something different, wearing red!"

"By the way, Jacob, I love you in the sports jacket. Where did you find it?"

"I had Sasha pick it up for me this afternoon."

"Sasha knows your size and your taste? Any other personal information she knows about you? She is quite helpful to you, isn't she?"

"Helpful, but just a friend—a lovely friend."

"Listen! Is that Michael Buble? That's my favorite vocalist."

"Let's dance, Lady Sara."

"I would love to dance, Master Donnithorne." I was swept from my chair and escorted to a small area just off the dining room. Jacob took me into his arms as though we were floating. The music ended. We returned to the table. The flight of reds was waiting. Jacob moved one of the wine carafes to my place setting.

"Try the Pinot Noir first. It's a light red with flavors of cranberry, cherry, and raspberry. It's called the crowd-pleaser because it goes with almost anything. It pairs well with salmon or richer meat like duck. Next is a Merlot. It is a medium red, soft like chocolate. The prominent flavors are blueberry, black currant, and cherry. Then, Cabernet Sauvignon, hearty and complex. Its predominant flavors are black cherry, blackberry, and currant. It has a peppery finish. And last, but not least, the Syrah which is a dark red wine with flavors of blackberry, blueberry, and currant. It offers a punch of flavor with hints of tobacco and allspice."

"You know so much about wine, Jacob."

"I have friends, the Damskeys, who are wine experts. They own Palmeri Wines in California. Check out Palmeri Wines on the internet. Kerry Damskey helped start the biggest winery in India. It's called Sula. Sula exports to the UK, and they have amazing reds and whites! We should go together to enjoy them, starting at Palmeri, and then on to Sula in India!"

"I find that so intriguing. Many men in farming country are limited to football, beer, cars, and women—not especially in that order, of course." Jacob and I laughed at the same time.

"When I moved to Worthing, I was delighted to find there were nerds like me who loved books, theater, and music. You are multi-layered, Jacob Donnithorne."

"Is there any other way, Sara Beck? It is what I like most about you. I chuckled when I saw you had been in my room, and then again when I saw you in the bathrobe and boots waiting for the cab. And that funny look on your face when you opened the bathroom door on the plane. Did you know you left a face print on the plane window?

"That's quite enough, Jacob. If you don't stop, we will be arguing like brother and sister again."

"Just trying to say, I love every crazy thing about you, Sara. You make me laugh, you irritate me, you pique my interest in so many ways."

"How sweet of you to say, Jacob."

"Do you know how many times I've stayed at the Griff, and I never once asked about the author who used to live here? You brought out the George Eliot in me, or should I say the George Lewes!"

"That's remarkable—I mean that you never once asked about George Eliot! There's a plaque in the entrance."

"Are you making fun of me? You're the journalist. I'm in real estate. We have different priorities. But that doesn't mean I'm not interested in what interests you."

"That is delicious, Jacob." I tipped my glass of Cabernet. "Very tasty. Spicy. I like it."

"I thought you would. Many women like whites because they've been told it is a lady's wine. Reds are mysterious, sexy, complex. Who wants white when a robust red titillates the palate?"

Jacob summoned the waiter. He delivered our menus, announced the du jour soups and salads, and stood with a linen towel over his arm waiting for our order.

"I would like the Beefeater house steak with the du jour soup and salad. What would you like, Sara?"

"I'm not typically a heavy eater, but that sounds inviting. I will have the same please."

"Two Beefeater steaks, du jour soups, and salads."

"Excuse me, Sara." Jacob walked over toward the bar. He whispered to the bartender and handed him money. I saw the bartender shake his head and walk toward the digital CD player above the bar.

"What did you do, Jacob?"

"This," he said, taking my hand and walking me to the dance floor. Suddenly in the background was Chris DeBurgh singing, Lady in Red. Jacob stared at me until I felt lightheaded with joy. Who needed wine? Who needed steak dinner? I wanted to dance all night in Arthur's—I mean Jacob's arms.

Back to Business

Chapter 23

The morning sun over Griff brought the neighboring rooster to waken me. It was a new day, a new world, perhaps even a new me. Folding my hands behind my head, I stayed in bed just long enough to dwell on last night's highlights: music, wine, dancing, Jacob dressed in a natural linen sports coat over jeans. I saw him in my mind walking to the bar to request the DeBurgh song for our dance. I'd noticed his long legs and lean body before, but not in the same way. Last night, he was divine. All of the previous days of his verbal torment were gone. His ego—my ego melted away in the soft glow of candlelight on our table. This must be how it felt for Marian and George Lewes.

A ring from my phone disturbed the quiet in my room. "Good morning, Mr. Cooper!"

"What's good about it, Beck?"

"Everything!"

"Have you been drinking?"

"Mr. Cooper, I'm not a drinker really. I have a glass of white wine at home while I'm waiting for dinner, and sometimes when I'm listening to Michael Buble."

"But?"

"But I shared a flight of reds with Mr. Donnithorne at dinner last night."

"Well doesn't that sound all cozy! Look, Beck, I have work for you to do over there. I need you to check the timeshares, and while you are at Griff, have a look around, sniff out a story, get plenty of photos."

"Yes, Mr. Cooper!"

"Back to reality, Beck. You are on salary over there, and you owe me for the wired cash advance."

"What angle do you want on the story?"

"Leaving that to you, but maybe something like The Protagonist Comes Unhinged!"

"Really, Mr. Cooper!"

"Take your time, Beck. Go south and see Stratford, Salisbury, Devon…."

The phone disconnected, and once again I was left with that "dismissive father" feeling. I shook it off and walked around the room basking in the memories of last evening. Could I be falling in love? Is this how true love felt?

"Are you coming to breakfast, Sara?" came Jacob's voice from the hallway.

"I'll be down soon. Start without me."

"I loved last night." Jacob's footsteps faded. Why didn't I answer him—affirm him?

"Lady in red is dancing with me cheek to cheek." I sang as if I was the only one in the hotel, and not even the morning maids could hear me. I was smitten.

"Ma'am, would you like your room tidied?" inquired the maid through the closed door.

"Not right now, thank you." No intrusions—none! I drew a bath, all the while singing aloud the song that described my enchanting moments with Jacob.

I put on the clothes that Jacob had loaned me the first morning at Griff. The red bolero jacket looked smart over top. The outfit could use a hat. It would have to do—this makeshift look—until I could shop for something else.

"Wow!" Love the jacket. All you need is a red hat to finish the look." I wasn't sure if Jacob was making fun of me or giving me a compliment. In any case, I was glad he noticed me.

"Thanks. Have you eaten yet?"

"Yes, I had French toast with back bacon like they served at Rosehill. By the way, did you feel chills going up your spine when the cab driver was pointing out the property where the Coventry Rosehill house used to be? I wonder if there is a connection?"

"I'm going to find out, Jacob. Mr. Cooper wants me to do some investigating. He called me this morning. I will start with Sasha's memorabilia, and move on from there."

"Great! I was just going to tell you that I need some time to do my business around the Midlands. Perhaps this morning we can go our separate ways and get some work done." My heart began to sink, though I knew it was the right thing to do. Part of me wanted to remain at Jacob's side.

"Sure, sure, that works for me!"

"I love that about you, Sara?"

"What's that?"

"You're independent."

I ordered eggs over easy, back bacon, grilled tomato with cracked pepper, buttered mushrooms, a scone, and strong black tea. Jacob got another cup of coffee while I ate. For some reason, I was as hungry as I'd ever been.

Pushing back from the table, I walked over to Jacob and gave him a quick kiss on the cheek. "I may or may not be back at Griff tonight. Mr. Cooper wants me to travel south out of the Midlands to take care of some business for him. I'll ask at the desk for them to hold my room until I get back."

"I'll be traveling too. I'll keep up with you by phone." Jacob rose from his chair and followed me out of the dining room. "You sure looked great in that red dress last night!"

"Thanks, Jacob." I left it there, feeling rather dismissive. His comment about liking my independence had left me feeling cold. Why didn't I just say I wanted to be with him? I walked back to my room to review the Griff history.

Sasha had provided me with a foot-high stack of magazines, books, photographs, and travel guides about the Griff and its halcyon days as the homestead of young Mary Anne Evans aka George Eliot. I fished through the stack and found a light yellow book, small in size, but big on facts. It was filled with photographs of Griff, Mary Anne, her family and friends, and yes, even George Lewes. I sank into the luxurious bed and immersed myself in George Eliot. The black and white photos of Lewes were exactly as I remembered him at Rosehill. And the one photo of Eliot was pretty scary— how I'd seen her that first night in the library. I read on to acquaint myself with Eliot's friends who influenced her ideas about religion. I found a picture of Sara Hennell, Mary Anne's close friend of twelve years. I read that she was a mystical, undisciplined writer who worked as a governess. So this was Sara, George Eliot's friend she compared with me.

Near the beginning of the book was a sketch of Rosehill, the Coventry haven for Mary Anne as well as other writers and philosophers from around the globe. The house looked so much like the Rosehill B & B!

I wondered about Jacob—where he was—what he was doing. I shook it off, and went back to what Mr. Cooper called sniffing for a story.

There was another photo of the Coventry area. The caption read "Coventry—our first vision in 1833." Sara Hennell wrote the information on the back of the water color she'd painted. Sara and Cara were sisters who had lived together at Rosehill. When Mary Anne Evans first visited, Sara had already become a governess, returning to Rosehill frequently for visits. In other words, Mary Anne and Sara were kindred spirits seeking out each other's company in spite of the odds. Mary Anne was a serious thinker, weighing information carefully before coming to a decision. On the other hand, Sara was spontaneous and undisciplined. Opposites attracted. The same thing happened between Marian and me at the Rosehill B & B.

There was a drawing of George Lewes in the back of the book. He looked wizened, just as I remembered him at Rosehill. A photo of a sprawling country home, captioned The Heights at Witley, revealed just how extravagant a lifestyle the two Georges had lived. Unfortunately, Lewes was not well enough to entertain many guests, and passed away shortly after they moved into the Heights near Haslemere. I would research to see if this palatial house was still standing. I wasn't sure exactly what Mr. Cooper was looking for, but I would fax what I had to date.

I stood up, stretched, and walked to the end of the hall to see if Sebastian, the cat, had gone in. He had.

There was movement at the front of the building. I peered down over the main hotel entrance and saw a group of people gathered. There was a man of medium height, with thinning hair and glasses addressing the group. He wore casual slacks over which a blue striped sweater was drawn. He seemed very comfortable leading a tour.

My curiosity got the better of me. I walked downstairs to see what was happening. The George Eliot Fellowship was touring the front area of Griff where the fireplace and office were located. I took a seat at the bar and waited for them to file in. I blended as though I was part of the group.

I learned that the leader's name was John Burton, the chair of The George Eliot Fellowship. He seemed very knowledgeable about the history of Griff and young Mary Anne. At his side was the vice chair, Vivienne Wood. She chimed in now and then to share her thoughts. They looked like two proud teachers introducing a school play. They looked out over the group, taking questions. I hurriedly moved away before I was discovered.

I bought one of those Beefeater burgers for lunch, and carried it back to my room. Digging deeper into the stack of memorabilia, I found a photo of the Griff brick kitchen oven. There appeared to have been some recent renovation, hence the discovery of the brick oven. I would follow-up with Sasha about it. After several hours of sorting and taking notes, I called Mr. Cooper to tell him I would be faxing what I had.

"Don't stop now, Beck! Keep moving on this. George Eliot is big right now, and call me crazy, but I think she's sniffing you out at the same time you are investigating her."

"I'm going to hop a cab and go down to Stratford for dinner, Mr. Cooper. I'm told that the bakery shops are lovely there. I may take in a play at the theater, maybe visit the grave of Shakespeare in the church south of town."

"Brilliant, Beck! You should travel to the places Eliot may have traveled. Have a pint for me at one of the pubs."

"That's not what George Eliot would have done, Mr. Cooper! I wouldn't walk into a pub by myself anyway."

"What happened to your Donnithorne buddy?"

"I'm on my own today. He's back to business too."

"Beck, you're a cold fish!"

"Mr. Cooper, I'm hanging up now!" It was the first time I'd hung up on Mr. Cooper."

The phone rang. I looked at the number. It was Mr. Cooper. I picked up the phone only to hear him hang it up on me! He was my nemesis. But what an intuitive thing for him to say about George Eliot investigating me. That was deep.

Fresh Air

Chapter 24

I had to get away from the Griff for a while. After I faxed my notes to Mr. Cooper from the front desk office, I called a cab. It felt good to be outdoors in the fresh spring air at the Griff. While I waited, I looked around taking in the sights and sounds. There was a freeway nearby, and I could hear the laughter of children mixed with birdsong. A squirrel sat in one of the ancient trees chewing through a nut shell. Except for the motorway, and its modern sounds, one could turn the clock back to the nineteenth century. It was surreal. The clouds covered the Midlands most days, and today was no different.

I pulled out my camera and shot some photos of attic rooms on the historical Griff house side. There was Sebastian, the resident cat, walking to and fro under the attic windows. A beam of light shot down on the split seam roofing just over the attic area. I was sure I'd caught it with my camera. The sun was playing tricks—there and gone in a moment.

The cab was on time. The driver was happy to have a large fare down to Stratford. He promised to come if I called him back before 6:00 P.M. I napped during the drive, waking only long enough to hear the two-way radio spitting out information on fares.

"Here we are, ma'am."

I got out at the side of town where the tourist information booth was located, and walked to it.

"Can I help you with something, ma'am"

"I would like to tour the theater, the Holy Trinity Church, and get some supper."

"There is a fine restaurant right over there." The ticket agent pointed to a very old establishment that looked upscale. He said their menu is traditional with pork pies being their specialty. You can get a pint there, ma'am, and fine wine too."

"Thank you, sir. I'll walk over to the theater first, and then along the Avon River down to the church to see Shakespeare's grave. I've heard it is under the floor. Do I pay for a ticket here?"

"Oh, no ticket needed for that, ma'am. You can just walk there from here. There are bus tours, but they are over for the day. Come at 9:00 A.M. tomorrow. You can see everything from the top of the bus, including the Shakespeare house and the thatched roof cottage of his wife, Anne Hathaway. Shakespeare walked from Stratford all the way to her country house to court her. Worth your time and money to see it."

"Thank you, sir. Until tomorrow then." I started across the tourist walkway to the theater, deciding to bypass it, and walk to the more interesting graveyard and Holy Trinity Church bordered by the Avon River.

"The church is closed today, ma'am. We have a choral group performing. Come tomorrow."

"I won't be here tomorrow, but thank you anyway."

"Here's a free pamphlet about Holy Trinity Church and Shakespeare's grave under the altar. He was buried here in 1616."

"Thank you." There was no chance they could close the Avon River, so I strolled down to the bank and wound my way back up to the theater. People were out everywhere enjoying the spring weather, and feeding the swans that were brave enough to come ashore. This is how I had always pictured England.

This historical gem—Stratford Upon Avon—had, for the most part, not changed a lot since young Mary Anne Evans visited with Emerson back in the mid-1800s. How exciting it must have been for her to travel from Coventry in the same carriage with such an esteemed philosopher, and to see a Shakespeare play in Stratford. I can imagine the philosophical conversations that were shared. What a lifelong impression Emerson must have left on the young lady.

I watched intently as the black and white swans crossed in pairs to meet the lovers on the opposite bank. It was an epiphany moment—like when you stand looking at a painting of lovers in Paris, and suddenly you realize what love is all about. Lovers choose to be together because they don't feel complete without one another. Even the romantic Avon River was less impressive when one was alone. I walked on.

The historical restaurant was in my view, and I had a mind to try one of the pork pies. There was dining inside and out, but those guests outdoors were leaning in and hugging. Every once in a while, laughter would break out from one of the bistro tables under the strung lights. My place was inside at a single table.

"May I get you a beverage, ma'am." The waiter was one of those ruggedly handsome types though his looks were softened by a bow tie and vest. His crisp white apron made him look very professional.

"Please, yes. White wine?"

"Sula Chenin Blanc all right?"

"Oh yes, I've heard Sula wines are excellent. And some chips please."

"Do you mean crisps, ma'am?"

"Oh, that's right, you call them crisps here, not potato chips as we do in the U.S."

"I'll be right back, ma'am."

I spotted a market guide pinned by the salt and pepper shakers. In it were shops and businesses around town. I was determined to visit a few of them before sundown.

"Can you tell me where this shop is, sir?" The waiter pointed to an adjacent street just beyond the tourist center.

"It is quite popular: magazines, newspapers, candy, toys. Most tourists walk there just to get a photo out front."

"I'll have the pork pie, please. Your house special I hear."

"It is, ma'am. Brilliant choice." He set the flute of Chenin Blanc down and smiled at me. "Most folks drink a pint here, but I see you have class. I'm a red wine drinker myself."

"Is that a man thing?"

"I wouldn't say it is a "man thing" but men seem to prefer reds to whites. Whites are preferred by women. The reds are sexy, complex, multi-layered...." I was almost sorry I asked. Jacob had insisted on red wine last night. I was open to it. I was feeling like red wine in that sassy red dress. I tried the Sula Chenin Blanc. It was delightful.

The pork pie was excellent. It was exciting sitting in a historical establishment overlooking the stunning Avon River eating traditional British fare. I jotted down some notes so that I could share with Mr. Cooper.

I had an hour to look around before sunset, so I walked to the quaint news store across the street. I bought some roll candies and a magazine, and headed into town. Some streets were very narrow with tiny shop windows filled with baked goods, candies, tea, and fine china.

Each storefront was a feast for the eyes. The bakery was my favorite. I stood staring into the window for several moments. Finally I stepped inside and bought shortbread cookies, blueberry scones, and some black tea to drink in my room at the Griff. I wandered back to the street where the cab driver had dropped me off. I fished out his business card and called the number.

"Too late. No more fares that far out."

"What should I do? I need to get back to Nuneaton."

"You can call a local cab and see if he will take you up there, but he will charge extra after hours. The only alternative is to stay the night in Stratford. There's a nice little hotel just across the street from where you are standing. They serve a fine breakfast too."

"Thank you very much, sir."

I got my bearings and walked across the street to the hotel. It overlooked the restaurant where I'd eaten dinner. I checked with the clerk about a room.

"One left, a double room. Would you like it, ma'am?"

"I have no choice. Yes." I signed in with the promise of cash payment in the morning.

"Want us to carry your luggage up, ma'am?"

"I have no luggage, just this briefcase. I didn't intend to stay the night in Stratford, but my cab driver is off duty, and I'm feeling a bit tired after walking all day."

The room was lovely with a brewing pot, a bathtub as well as shower, and there were two double beds that were well appointed. I hunted for the phone charger and plugged my drained phone into the unit. Happy to be inside a safe room, and thrilled to have tea bags and treats from the British bakery, I settled in and began the slow descent to the bottom of the bakery bag.

Once my phone was charged, I called Mr. Cooper to tell him I'd gotten stranded in Stratford overnight.

"If one has to be stranded, that's the place for it. Enjoy your stay, Beck."

"Mr. Cooper—?" He was gone. I just needed someone to talk to even if it was grumpy Mr. Cooper. I flipped on the television and heard the Prime Minister delivering a speech to Parliament. It all seemed so formal here in England.

I fell asleep at 9:00 P.M., neglecting a bath and wearing a hotel robe in lieu of pajamas. I didn't realize how exhausted I was.

My phone rang at 11:00 P.M. I picked it up, and perked up when I heard Jacob's voice.

"Where are you, Sara? I've been waiting here all night for you."

"You have? Why?"

"Why? Isn't that a silly question?"

"No. I told you I might sleep at a hotel other than Griff tonight."

"Yes, you did say that, but I was hoping to hear from you to let me know you were all right. Where are you?"

"I'm at a small hotel just across from the Royal Shakespeare Theatre in Stratford."

"I'll be right there." He was gone before I could protest.

I began to panic. There were no more rooms! I ran to take a bath and brush out my hair. I put the hotel robe back on, tucked the sheets, replaced the hotel spread, and arranged the bolster. I cleaned up the bakery bag and the roll candy wrappers. I brewed tea in the little hotel pot.

I sat nervously on the edge of the bed. He was on his way—for what? Would he try to drive me back to Griff? Would he insist on staying in my room? Heaven help me! There was a lobby downstairs with comfy couches; he could sleep there! In my mind I heard Chris DeBurgh singing Lady in Red, and I felt my cheeks begin to blush.

Swans on the Avon

Chapter 25

I guessed from the knocking at the door, it must be Jacob. I looked through the peephole to find it was the desk clerk waiting for me to answer. What could she want this time of night?

"Ma'am, a gentleman who says he knows you is waiting in the lobby. Since he is not a registered guest, I could not give him your room number. Would you like him to come up?"

"No, I will go down to greet him."

"In your robe, ma'am?"

"I'll dress. Give me five minutes."

"By the way, ma'am, your room phone is off the hook. I tried to ring you, but it was busy for some time."

"My apologies. I must have bumped the receiver when I made the bed."

Hurriedly I put my clothes back on, and dashed for the elevator. I pushed the ground floor button, and stepped inside. When it stopped, my heart was pounding.

I pushed the second floor button again. The elevator bumped back to the upper floor. I decided to take the stairs so that I had time to compose myself. Walking as though I had not a care in the world, I made my way into the lobby. Jacob was sitting in a high back chair wearing a classy new overcoat.

"Sasha pick up more clothes for you, Jacob?"

"No, Sara. I went shopping in London today—well, yesterday now." He looked down at his watch to confirm the time as 12:30 A.M. "I took the train. I shopped for us."

"Us?"

"Don't sound shocked. Sara, you've held two outfits of mine hostage for days! Time for something new and fresh. Do you think I could ever wear my—your trousers again with a straight face?"

"They look much better on you, Jacob. Thank you for thinking of me."

"My pleasure." He lifted several packages up from the floor, and opened a large, blue rectangular box. I gulped. Then I laughed out loud when I saw a Calvin Klein raincoat—in red! "It has a hood too! You'll need it trouncing around England, Sara."

"I love it. Thank you! I see you like red."

"On you, I love red, Sara."

"What's in the other boxes?"

"I'll show you tomorrow. Now let's get some sleep. Your eyes are baggy."

"Baggy? And how are we going to sleep with you here?"

"What do you mean? We are in a hotel. People sleep here."

"Funny fellow, aren't you? Well, I took the last room in the place. Had you not rudely hung up on me, I could have told you that when you were sitting at the Griff."

"No, really? Now what will we do?" Jacob looked perplexed. "I know, I'll camp out with you."

"Oh no!"

"No?"

"How would it look, Jacob?"

"Who's watching? That hotel clerk? Night security? Ok, look, I see how uptight you are about all of this. I will sleep elsewhere."

"Elsewhere? It's after midnight, and you have all of those packages."

"I'll leave the packages with you, and I will get a cab to another hotel."

Jacob walked to the hotel desk. "Ma'am, could you check for a hotel for me at another location?"

"What is your preference?"

"Anything right now."

"Give me a moment." Five minutes passed, and finally the clerk looked up from her phone list. "I'm afraid there's nothing, Mr. Donnithorne. There is an Air B & B available if you are in their system."

"I am."

"Let me ring up the number for you." She handed the phone across the desk.

"Yes, this is Jacob Donnithorne. I need a place to stay for the night. There was a pause, and then Jacob shook his head and responded to the voice on the other end. "Perfect. I'll be right there." He turned to the hotel clerk and thanked her profusely.

"Sara, get your things. I will call a cab for us."

"Say what?"

"I rented an entire house for us. There are three bedrooms. With locking doors—ok?"

I broke into a huge smile and ran to the elevator. The hotel room on the second floor looked somehow sad as I gathered my briefcase and personal items, and raced downstairs.

Jacob stood by the revolving hotel door, holding boxes and bags. I took a few of his packages, and smiled up at him. He'd been a real gentleman. There weren't many like him left.

"There's our cab; let's go."

"Wait, I have to pay my bill!"

"It's paid. No worries."

"Oh, Jacob, you didn't have to do that."

"I know."

We stuffed the trunk of the cab with packages, and away we trundled through the ancient streets of Stratford where Shakespeare had walked—where literary greats from all walks of life had gathered to meet him and watch his plays—where Eliot sat in the theater seat next to Ralph Waldo Emerson, America's Transcendental philosopher. Here—here was heaven—tucked into the bricked streets of Stratford with its little shops of dainty pink tea cakes, its restaurants featuring authentic British pork pies, the Avon River rolling south to Severn.

"What are you dreaming about now, Sara?"

"This is a dreamy night, Jacob, and we're in one of the quaintest cities in England. Have you read any Shakespeare?"

"I studied Shakespeare in college."

"Do tell! I've always wanted to study Shakespeare."

"It was just a summer seminar with a professor who knew Shakespeare inside out. He'd been at the college for nearly fifty years."

"How is that possible for a professor to be at one institution that long?"

"He was tenured, and he loved teaching. Students were more important to him than the politics of the college."

"That's dedication. Will you read from Shakespeare for me Jacob?"

"I'll do one better, I will take you to a play in the Royal Shakespeare Theatre."

"Oh, Jacob, I can't wait!" I lay my head against the window of the cab, watching the lights of the town shoot by.

"Lay your head on my shoulder, Sara. That window is cold. I leaned over against Jacob's crisp new overcoat, and fell asleep.

The next thing I knew I was being carried into a room. I felt Jacob's strong arms around me as he lay me down into a bed. His hand brushed the hair from my forehead. I felt the ivory boots from Rosehill leave my feet.

The bedroom door closed, and I felt totally safe, secure, and loved for the first time in my life. I rolled over, gathered the pillows and pressed them against me, hugging them like they were so many children. In the outer room, I heard Jacob humming as he switched off the lights and went to bed. "To sleep perchance to dream…."

The Heights

Chapter 26
Dream

I was in a large, storied house filled with dark, marble-top Victorian furniture. A man was fiddling with his pocket watch. He turned and saw me watching him, and addressed me as Marian. I tried to tell him I was not Marian. He was having none of it.

"Perhaps some brandy, Marian. You've been working on your new manuscript so long that you've become delirious."

"Yes, a bit of brandy, George." The man walked to a table in the far corner of the room.

"The room is so large. I'm thankful the staff came ahead of us and warmed it with our belongings. Our walls of books define us—hold us together in literary love." Had I said that, or had Marian? Maybe we both said it. Was I awake inside a dream?

"Yes, Marian. We do need our comforts." He walked toward me with a snifter of brandy. The facets in the crystal shone like Christmas candles. "Is your water bottle warm enough?   I looked to see what George Lewes was pointing at. There was a thick rubber bag under my feet. It was warm and comforting.

"It's fine. Sit with me and read."

"Let me adjust your footstool." He lifted my foot and began to massage it with his small hands. "Would you like me to remove your house booties?" He unbuttoned the familiar ivory boots. Why was I—Marian—being showered with attention?

"Shall I call Mary to bring you a warm wrap?"

"Call Charlotte. She's on night duty. Mary is resting after a long day of arranging the new kitchen." He rang a bell on the corner panel near the doorway. Charlotte came padding up the long staircase.

"Charlotte, dear, would you get Mrs. Lewes a warm wrap?"

"Yes, sir." She curtsied and left the room.

"Marian, I hated the long wait getting into the Heights, but it is June, and here we are, and the roses are blooming. Let us walk about tomorrow."

"That sounds lovely. I can't think of anything else I would rather do—except walk along the Avon River and pretend to be the swans."

"Oh? So now you want to go to Stratford? I'm not sure my health is up to the coach ride, Marian."

"No worries, we can play black swan-white swan another time, my love."

"Let's stay close to home for now. The fresh air of Witley will do us both good. Travel has worn us down. And Bath seemed to do little good for either of us. Personally, I think their healing springs are over-rated. When I am well, we should travel down to the Wiltshire Plains again—stay in that quaint B & B you liked so much. Plenty of fresh air there."

"Indeed, Wiltshire sounds lovely. But we must not overtax you. The doctor said you needed rest and recuperation. When you are well enough, we will go. Now sit, George, and read to me."

"What would you like me to read, Marian?"

"The *Daniel Deronda* reviews please." George looked nervous.

"I haven't read them myself yet, Marian. The news clippings are on my desk."

"I'm anxious to hear how the book is doing."

"Tomorrow, my love. Tonight let us nestle together and read Shakespeare." He drew up a chair, opened an antiquated personal volume, flipped the pages to the sonnets section, and began to read. I settled back into the button-tufted chair and listened, every now and then looking at the little man who was totally devoted to me. Suddenly he winced in pain.

"I'm sorry, Marian, I can no longer sit. There is too much discomfort."

Partners in Mischief

Chapter 27

The smell of bacon filled my room. I woke to find a breakfast tray at my bedside. For a moment, I thought I was back at Rosehill—God forbid! I looked around and smiled when I remembered that Jacob had brought us to this lovely Air B & B. Who served me breakfast? I chomped on bacon and drank some of the rich, black tea. There was a bell at my bedside. I rang it to see if a maid would come. In popped Jacob. He was holding a glass of orange juice. I sat up in bed, pulling the covers around me like a clam shell.

"Good morning, Sara!"

"Morning, Jacob. I was ringing for the maid."

"There is no maid. Just you and me."

"Thank you for this lovely breakfast, Jacob. But where did you get the food?"

"It was in the refrigerator. This is almost like having a home away from home. Did you rest well?"

"I did, but I had this strange dream. I was watching the characters in the dream, but I was also one of those characters!"

"Sounds like lucid dreaming to me."

"Oh? And what is lucid dreaming?"

"It is when you are awake inside a dream and know that you are dreaming. You are interacting within the dream. Often you remember details of the dream once you wake up."

"Fascinating!"

"What was your dream about?"

"Well, there was a lady sitting in a chair with her feet propped on a footstool. She was wearing the ivory leather boots I wore at Rosehill."

"…and beyond!" Jacob interrupted.

"The man, who seemed like her husband, was anxious to please her—to meet her every need."

"That was a fantasy, not a dream!" Jacob laughed out loud.

"May I continue?"

"Sorry. Yes, go ahead; I won't interrupt again."

"The lady's name was Marian, and she'd just published a new novel. What was the name of that? Let me think—oh yes, it had Daniel in it—*Daniel Deronda*. The novelist wanted the man to read her the reviews, and he begged off. He was hiding something."

"What was the setting? Where were you?"

"The man, a short, frumpy fellow whom she called George, was talking about the move to their big house. It was the month of June, and they were still making things comfortable. He brought her a snifter of brandy, and read Shakespeare to her until he was obviously experiencing pain. Something about his sitting position was making him uncomfortable. I saw that they were surrounded by books—walls of books."

"How did that dream make you feel?"

"In many ways, it made me feel secure, loved, and sad that the man who seemed like my own husband was not feeling well. Apparently the two of them were bonded as one, enjoying their lives in every respect. I know it was just a dream, but it was a personal dream. I hope the man gets well so they can travel again."

"Did you recognize the characters—did they seem familiar?" Jacob was genuinely interested.

"As a matter of fact, they looked like Marian and George in the Rosehill library—the couple who wanted me to travel to England with them. Do you remember her? She wore a black veil over her head. She read her own novels in the library each night. The guests adored her. The little man, named George, was always fussing over her. He was the socialite of the two. Most found him overbearing and obnoxious, but Marian apparently loved him dearly."

"I vaguely remember them. I wasn't there long. Well, they let you down. They didn't travel to England with you. I did."

"Yes, and I daresay that your early company was as bad as George Lewes' might have been on a trip!"

"He was that bad?" Jacob laughed and picked up the tray from my bedside table.

"You acted sarcastic and egotistic on purpose?"

"Of course. It's what most guys do when they are not sure a lady is interested. They test around to see if they will stay."

"And if they do—stay?"

"Then they take them out to dinner, buy them a flight of wine, preferably reds, and dance with them to alluring music."

"You can stop there! Just how many times have you done this, Jacob?"

"More times than I care to admit, Sara. But relax, I'm older now, and I'd like to find someone who will ignite my passions for travel and mystery. You, Sara Beck, are different—so different from the others I've known.

"Be careful, Jacob, I might write a book about you!"

"Oh, you write books too?"

"Well, the lady in my dream, whose boots I've worn, writes novels. Who knows?"

Jacob slipped through the door, and re-entered with the packages he'd loaded and unloaded the night before.

"Here, take a look. I had a clerk help me choose them." I opened one of the boxes to find a lovely pink day dress that had large pockets and a belted waistline. Another package held a simple pair of leather walking sandals.

"Perfect for touring!"

"That is exactly what the lady at Bloomingdale's said."

"Bloomingdale's?"

"Yes, I get discounts there. Open the round box."

I picked up the tall round box. Inside was a lovely straw hat with a spray of light pink rosebuds on a white band. "Oh, you are spoiling me, Jacob!" He handed me a small rectangular package. It was a pair of sunglasses like Audrey Hepburn made famous.

"The clerk said these were a must have item for any fashionable traveling lady. Try them on." I slid the over-sized glasses behind my ears, set the hat atop my head and looked up at Jacob.

"Well, maybe they will look better with the dress."

"I'm going for a bath, Jacob. I can't wait to pull the outfit together. Thank you!"

"The Air B & B owners have provided us with organic honey products. I tried them myself. I feel pure somehow!" Jacob joked.

"Now *that* is funny!" Our laughter locked itself together like a pair of scissor blades cutting through the monotony of life.

"Hurry, so we have plenty of time to enjoy the day. The sun is shining! That's a rare British experience."

I was giddy with excitement. "What play will we see at the theater?"

"*The Taming of the Shrew.*"

"Very funny. Really, what play?"

"*The Taming of the Shrew!*" Jacob laughed out loud and walked through the door with my tray. Any retort after that would be useless. He was enjoying the moment too much to hand me the controls.

The bathroom had a sunken marble tub. Who lives like this? I ran a steaming bath and added honey bath syrup. Interesting name for a bath product. It almost smelled edible too. As I lay there soaking in luxury, I thought of the honey bees that had come to our childhood home in the 1980s. I watched them swarm, then go into a hollow tree in the front yard. I spent most of that summer watching the bees build a hive. They didn't mind my being there. I think they sense who is trustworthy and who is not.

"Are you all right in there? It's been thirty minutes. We'll be late for the play."

"Give me fifteen more minutes."

I climbed out of the sunken tub and looked back with regret that I could not stay longer. The morning sun was peeping through stained glass windows set over the double sinks. I wrapped myself in a cotton robe and looked for a toothbrush. There was a fresh brush and a sample size toothpaste inside the vanity cabinet. The owners had thought of everything.

In the bathroom, I dressed quickly in my pink day dress, I slipped on the tan leather sandals and straw hat, and ran to meet Jacob in the kitchen.

"Your sunglasses, Sara?"

"Almost forgot." I walked to the bedroom and found the bed made and room tidied. The glasses were sitting on top of my briefcase.

"Did you make the bed, Jacob?"

"Who else?"

"Thank you. I'm not used to such royal treatment. When I was growing up, I learned to be independent. My mother and father were too busy with the younger twins. And being single most of my adult life has me regimented.

"Good!"

"Don't get any ideas, Jacob. I don't wait on men."

"But I'm waiting on you."

"True. And I love it!" I tried on the sunglasses.

"Oh, adorable you!"

"Let's go!" I grabbed my briefcase and headed for the door.

"Really? A briefcase on a summer picnic kind of day?" Jacob looked at me in disapproval. "Let's get you a snappy shopping bag to carry! They are in vogue right now. Famous designers make them.

"How sheek!" I set the case down and took Jacob's arm. It felt good.

"Now that's better." He put on his brightly banded straw hat, and out the door we went.

"Let's have our portrait done today. I would like to remember us in Stratford among the swans. What do you think, Jacob? I saw artists at the water's edge when I walked near Holy Trinity Church yesterday."

He answered with a smile.

Suddenly Shakespeare

Chapter 28

The theater was bustling with tourists. While we waited for the next play to start, we walked around the museum and gift shop. There were Shakespeare books, umbrellas, canes, greeting cards, candy, stuffed Shakespeare dolls in pantaloons—anything Shakespeare could be found in that shop!

"Here is the perfect bag for shopping," Jacob said, swinging the Shakespeare insult bag in front of me. It's canvas, so it's washable and very lightweight."

"Are you sure you are in real estate? You sound like a department store salesman!"

"Nah, just being cute."

"I like this one. Renoir's Luncheon of the Boating Party, 1881. And it goes with the pink day dress you bought for me."

"Aren't you the fashionista all of the sudden!"

"I learned from Calista, and from you, my benevolent gifter!"

"I owe everything I know about fashion to the ladies at Bloomingdale's of London!" Jacob admitted.

"I come from farming country, Jacob, and I grew up in blue jeans and t-shirts. We ladies wore dresses to church and dances, but other than that, we wore serviceable jeans and garden boots. This hat you bought me is a lovely sun hat, but it isn't suitable for gardening.

"I should get you something sturdier for gardening?" He said it in such a way that it seemed he was hiding something in plain sight."

"What do you mean, Jacob? I don't garden anymore."

He quickly changed the subject. "The Renoir bag it is!" He paid the cashier, and we hurried to our theater seats for *The Taming of the Shrew*. "Great seats if I don't say so myself."

"Yes, they are. I could almost reach out and touch their velvet pantaloons from here."

"I'm shocked, Miss Beck!"

"Just kidding."

"I thought so...." I got the idea he liked the Sara that wore red, dared to share a flight of wine, and could be a bit ornery on occasion. I was not that Sara, or was I?

"Shh...the Royal Shakespeare Company is coming on stage." Jacob opened the play bill and pulled out a pair of opera glasses. He offered them to me. I laughed out loud.

"Really? I can see perfectly well from here."

"You might want to get a close look at those velvet pantaloons, Sara." We broke into spontaneous laughter. The couple in front of us turned to register their disapproval.

The play begins with a brief synopsis of *Shrew*, and an introduction of Shakespeare's characters. Then from behind the curtains comes a drunken tinker named Christopher Sly. He has been thrown out of a Warwickshire alehouse. Enter a lord and his hounds and hunting party. They toy with the tinker. A young page disguises himself as the tinker's wife. "I am your wife in all obedience," she says.

"Shakespeare highlights human absurdities in his comedies. But *All's Well that Ends Well*."

"Very funny, Jacob."

"Shh!" The couple in front of us turned again and drilled us with their eyes.

The scene shifts to Italy where the shrew, Kate, finds herself with suitors. She refuses to marry, but marry she must before her younger sister, Bianca. In act III, Kate is carried away by Petruchio to his country house in Verona. There he is determined to make Kate submissive by withholding food and sleep—all with the best of husbandly intentions. Petruchio accompanies Kate back to Padua. The play ends with Kate attending her younger sister's public wedding, advising Bianca on her duties as a wife to Lucentio. Kate is unaware that they had been married earlier in a private ceremony.

"You see, *All's Well that End's Well!*"

"You can't seriously think that this "problem" play ended well, Jacob! It reminds me of the nightmare called Rosehill! They forbade me to enter common rooms, fed me less than I wanted at mealtime, ridiculed me at every turn. I felt subservient. And poor Marian trapped by that little man, Lewes. He managed her at every turn. I wish I had been able to help her."

"I'm sorry, Sara. It's just a Shakespeare comedy—a silly play. I have no plan to enslave you. Rosehill is over and done. My experience was different from yours, but I chose the modern period of Stephen King. The adjustment was much easier for me."

"Let's get out of here!" I jumped up from my seat and walked quickly toward the entrance. Jacob was close on my heels.

"Sara, I said I'm sorry. Wait!"

"I need to walk. Let's go down to the southwest bank of the Avon to the Holy Trinity Church."

"Let's. It sounds lovely. You know, Sara, the female students in the Shakespeare seminar I attended had the same reaction as you. The males all boasted like football players who had just won a game. But our professor told us that when two people pull together there is no need to tame one another."

"That professor expressed common sense for the modern couple. I should take that seminar myself."

"Look, Sara, there's an artist on the bank, and the swans are coming up to sun themselves. Let's ask if we can have a portrait painted."

"Jacob, this day is magical even if you took me to that dreadful play. You introduced me to Shakespeare. No man I've dated, and there have been several, has ever cared to go to the theater or read a book to discuss it with me. Marian enjoyed Shakespeare. Lewes read to her. They read to each other. Did you know that?"

"I don't know much about George Eliot. Only the things you've shared with me. We'll have to read together. Stephen King?"

"Let's start with Eliot, and if you have not met your match in her, then I will read Stephen King with you."

"Deal!"

"Please sit still so that I can get this portrait right. You are two perfect subjects—obviously in love—but you move too much for a novice painter like me." We sat like stone until the painter finished. He lifted his cute little head with its tousle of white hair. "The painting needs to dry, so if you have shopping or tourist activities, you may come back for this later."

"Perfect. Thank you, sir."

"You may call me Albert."

"Something about Albert looks very familiar, Jacob."

"Did you see him along the bank yesterday?"

"No." I looked back trying to place him. Nothing.

Jacob and I headed on foot along the bank of the Avon, climbed over a low fence, and walked into the Holy Trinity churchyard. "Shall we go inside to see Shakespeare's grave in the altar."

"I would love that. Now that I've been introduced to the town where he lived, and to one of his plays, the grave will seem more meaningful."

"This is much smaller than a cathedral. I once saw the famous Salisbury Cathedral. The spire is leaning far enough that it is visible to the naked eye. There's a copy of the Magna Carta there sealed behind glass."

"That's fascinating! You've traveled much more than I have, Jacob. I would love to see more of England."

"Scotland too?"

"Oh, yes. I would love to see where my ancestors lived. Aberdeen, a fishing port, I'm told. My family is somehow related to the Gordon clan."

"The Gordon clan—as in George Gordon, Lord Byron?"

"Impressed?"

"Indeed!"

"Don't be. He was a famous poet, and as you say a Lord, but he had the worst reputation with women. George Eliot disapproved of him. She wasn't pure as the driven snow, but George Gordon, Lord Byron was known as a blackguard."

"What is a blackguard?"

"A player. A man who uses a woman for what he can get. Lord Byron had a club foot. It is my belief that he tried to prove himself manly by wooing women with his wealth and romantic poetry, and then disposed of them to build his ego."

"That's quite an armchair analysis, Sara."

"It's subjective to my own life experience, I'm sure. I've known some blackguards in my time."

"Look at that amazing grave plaque. It's exciting to think that William Shakespeare's bones are under this altar!" Jacob exclaimed.

"Good old Will Shakespeare! His sweetheart's parents owned a farm with a thatched cottage. Young Will walked miles to see Anne often. They had the perfect landscape for falling in love: fresh country air, flower gardens, an orchard, and the romantic thatched cottage that even today draws people from around the world with its old world charm. Did you know that Anne was pregnant when they married? Will didn't behave well, but he was committed to Anne, unlike Byron's conquests and departures."

"Perhaps we should go see the cottage before leaving Stratford, Sara? It would seem fair since we are paying homage to her husband today." Jacob waited for my response.

"Yes, I'd venture to say that Anne was not a shrew that was tamed—not even by Will Shakespeare. I read somewhere that Anne assisted in her husband's writing. But she got no public credit for it, of course."

"Here lies the greatest writer who ever lived. He had a wife named Anne Hathaway. I wonder how different it might have been if Will had married another?"

"That's very sensitive of you, Jacob."

"We each have a life to live. We couple ourselves with friends, lovers, even parasites that suck the very life from us. It happens in the workplace, in social settings, even in our own homes. We must remember always, Sara, that we are individuals first, and coupled in life as a secondary option. Anne Hathaway lived in a time when women were servile to their men. Their value mainly consisted of keeping house and raising children. The women who didn't marry became governesses. Your George Eliot knew the Emersonian view of being an individual first, but I daresay that she enjoyed being a woman more than most—even if she did have a male pseudonym."

"Now look who is being the armchair psychologist! And waxing nostalgic about Emerson. You've come a long way on the banks of the Avon, Jacob."

"Wait until you see all of the tombs and plaques in the cathedrals around England. We can visit Salisbury Cathedral together if you like."

"Don't you have business to tend to, Jacob?"

"Yes, but I can beg off on it for a few days. We can visit the Hathaway cottage tomorrow, and then head to Bath. From there, the drive down to Salisbury is extraordinary! We can stay at The Red Lion and book a tour of Stonehenge—take the bus through the Wiltshire Plains."

"We'd better get our painting first, and find dinner. I ate at a quaint historical place right over there last night." I pointed in the general direction.

"Let's go back to the Air B & B first. We'll get our overcoats. It's a bit damp in this river town come evening."

• • •

"The portrait is more beautiful than I expected it to be. Your eyes are radiant under that sunhat, Sara. Thank you, kind sir. Albert is it?" The artist nodded and shook Jacob's hand. We'll look you up again."

"I'll be around." Albert said. I am known for hiding my name on my portraits. What seems hidden is right in front of our eyes. Thank you for this chance to be part of your beautiful lives. My brush doesn't lie."

Jacob handed me the painting. He leaned in close, pondering what Albert had said. I felt my heart racing without a word between us. Something magical was happening. Was it Albert—the artist that rarely looked up from his canvas. But when he did, his twinkling blue eyes were saying something. Who was he, and how did I know him?

"Good day to you then. I will be packing up before the evening chill gets in my bones." Albert set his brushes into a worn wood case that was spattered with pastel paints.

"Look, Jacob." I whispered.

"Poor Albert. His back must be in pain the way he is bent over like that. Scoliosis?"

"No," I whispered again. "It's a hump. He was born like that."

"How do you know? You are acting quite mysterious, Sara."

"I know him through Marian."

"You mean Marian Evans—George Eliot?"

"Yes, that's exactly who I mean. He's the artist that painted the famous portrait of her in the black velvet gown. He used his self-portrait and added to it. No one thought it looked like young Mary Anne, but Albert was trying to send her a message that she was beautiful inside just like him. The outer appearance is paint."

"That's deep, Sara. You should be a writer."

"I am, Jacob—a journalist."

"No, I mean—a novelist."

"I'm proud of what I do, but I've always wanted to write a book. Perhaps I'll do that when we get back to the States." We turned away from Albert and toward the northeast. Shakespeare's statue was to our left toward the center of the tourist walk. Let's do something to commemorate our visit to Stratford." We walked to the statue of William Shakespeare. I scribbled a note, rolled it into a scroll and tied it with the ribbon from my sunhat. I placed it at the statue.

"What does the note say?" Jacob asked.

"Here is a statue of my husband, William. He is all things to all people: poet, playwright, social butterfly, handsome devil…I could go on. Enjoy who he is because at his right hand was a strong woman who raised his children, kept his home, waited for him during his long absences, and even helped write and edit some of his plays. You could not have loved him better, but I have surely loved him best.
~ Anne Hathaway-Shakespeare"

"You amaze me more each moment I'm with you, Sara. That is as poetic as Shakespeare himself!"

"It flows like a river from within. Albert knows what I mean. Each person has a gift, no matter the handicap."

"That's interesting, Sara."

"I wear the mantle of women who struggle to be seen and heard for their efforts to succeed. Some, like Eliot, are happy to be at home, writing from their kitchen tables. Others want to be involved in a high-paced broadcast or newspaper scene. And there's the lady who edits quietly in the back office while big names get the credit. They've all managed to feed their kids, help pay the bills, and cover medical costs, but they live unfulfilled lives. I would like to reach out to them."

"The best way for you to do that, Sara, is to write for larger audiences. Write from your heart. Be heard. Don't die quietly working for a daily newspaper. That's why I...."

"That's why you what?" Jacob turned and walked away. Something was troubling him. He had a deep secret about his own life, and here I was going on about mine.

"It's beginning to rain." We ran as fast as we could back to the Air B & B, but my pink day dress still got soaked. Luckily the portrait stayed dry under Jacob's shirt. We shook like dogs fresh from a bath. "I'll put on some tea. You run a bath for yourself."

"That is so sweet, Jacob. Thank you. I'll be quick so that you have time to bathe too. Then we should find dinner somewhere. Now that you have encouraged me to experiment with food and drink, I think I could try almost anything, except squid or octopus! And no brains, or tripe, or...."

"All right, I get the point. Let's stay in tonight. We've been rushing since we left Rosehill. We can enjoy a leisurely bath, read, listen to music, have some wine, eat—wait, we have nothing to eat. I'll call a take-out restaurant. Go run your bath."

I felt blessed in every way for the first time in my life. I thought I'd known love, and even a bit of solitary happiness, but nothing like the moments alone with Jacob. The bath steam rolled up over me like billowing summer clouds. I closed my eyes, and fell asleep.

"Dinner is ready." It was Jacob in the outer room. I climbed out of the tub, put on a heavy robe, and wrapped my hair in a turban. I walked into the next room.

"I must have fallen asleep!"

"No worries. Everything is still piping hot. I love your dinner dress and matching hat!"

"It was the best I could do."

"How many times have I heard you say that since I first saw you looking me over in the Rosehill library, Sara?"

"You knew? Oh how embarrassing."

"Well, I'm not drop dead gorgeous, but I am pleasant looking enough. Women are drawn to my sandy hair and bright blue eyes."

"Hah, pleasant looking enough? You must be one of the most eligible bachelors in England!"

"Well, if I am, I'm unaware of it."

"You sound like Jane Austen's Elena in *Sense and Sensibility!* She said equally ridiculous things like, 'I do highly esteem him.' That was her description of her feelings for Mr. Ferrars. She was in love, but felt it unwise to say so too quickly. One must be sensible in all things, including love."

"Pull up your chair, Sara, and let's eat this Chinese shrimp with vegetables. I ordered wonton soup and egg rolls too. I have some chilled wine for us—a Chenin Blanc I found in London. The shop imports this label from Sula of India."

"I've had this one. It's delicious! You said your friends from California helped Sula start their winery in India. If they are shipping to England, they are doing quite well."

"We can enjoy it in front of the fireplace later." He handed me chopsticks. Lifting a clump of sticky rice with ease, he came up to my mouth with it. Next shrimp, then a water chestnut. The more he fed me, the more I felt like not eating. I felt nervous, like I was losing control. Finally he pulled back and ate from his box.

"You're staring," Jacob said.

"Yes, I am. So much serendipity: the rare day of sunshine in Stratford, the artist who had a clear message for us, this perfect little haven for us to eat and sleep with all the privacy we need. I feel that it all came together at the right time. I can be myself with you, Jacob."

"I feel the same with you, Sara." He leaned forward and dabbed brown sauce from my lips. I wanted him to kiss me just then—to take me into his arms and confess his love for me, but he didn't.

"Are you all right, Sara?"

"Oh—yes!"

"I'm going to get my bath now. Did you save me some honey bath syrup? I'll join you later at the fireplace for a glass of wine."

"That would be perfectly lovely."

Sense of Place

Chapter 29

Jacob joined me at the fireplace in his own thick cotton robe. I sat with my arms around my knees. Every move was an ache to hold him—to kiss him—to tell him I'd spent my life waiting for a fairytale version of him. I could not—I would not do so. The risk was too great, so I remained quiet and stared at the fire. He stared at the fire too as though inside those flames were the will to make us each dance to our desires.

"Wine?" He lifted the bottle of Chenin Blanc, and filled our glasses. When he'd poured his own, he held up his glass to propose a toast. "To us—to a beautiful friendship unfolding into something even more special than either of us had ever imagined." The glasses clinked. We sipped slowly. "Exquisite!"

"Jacob?"

"Yes?"

"Kiss me."

No additional words were needed. Jacob took our glasses and placed them on a stand near the fireplace. He leaned in and kissed me like this was his only chance to prove his passion. I could scarcely breathe. Every fiber of my being quivered.

"I love you," he said. I've tried to fight this. I know you have too. We've both been hurt. I've been slighted by overbearing women. You have been broken by overbearing men. We are at this juncture in our lives together because we bring healing to our deepest wounds." Jacob pulled me in and held me. "I will always be here for you. I will always be a gentleman. I will love you even if you say you don't love me back."

"You are too good to be true, Jacob Donnithorne. Of course I love you. I've known since the night you danced with me. At first I thought it was the music, the red wine, the way you held me as we danced. But it was the fact that you were a perfect gentleman when you had every opportunity to take advantage of me. Marian could not have been more wrong about you."

"It is not because I don't want to—take advantage, but I know how vulnerable you are. I know because I am vulnerable too. Hurt people are like sponges. They need and want love, and sometimes they allow themselves to be used because they don't feel worthy of being loved. Hurt people also create roadblocks to healthy relationships. They don't know how to operate in a healthy relationship. They fear failure."

"Sounds plausible," I said.

He brushed the hair from my face and pressed his cheek against mine. "Have we found our safe place with one another? Only time will tell, Sara. But for now, we have this exquisite soul-sense of one another's needs. Let's take it slowly. Let's learn how to live for and fulfill one another."

"While at Rosehill, I envied George Lewes and Marian Evans. I lived vicariously on scenes from her novels—like Hetty and Arthur Donnithorne in *Adam Bede*. I wanted to be Hetty and feel Arthur's arms around me, his lips passionately kissing mine. His breath heavy on my cheek. Eliot sure knew how to use restraint. There were several meetings between Adam Bede and Hetty, and Dinah and Adam Bede. But Adam was a perfect gentleman throughout. Hetty was as passionate as ripe fruit. Captain Arthur Donnithorne, with his air of entitlement, could not resist."

"Please give me an example of Adam's gentlemanly behavior," Jacob laughed.

"In one scene, Hetty was picking red currants from a bush, placing them into a small basket she held in the crook of her arm up against her bosom. She stopped picking momentarily, and ate one of the currants. Her lips were stained red. Her fingers were covered with currant juice. Adam had come to visit her while she was harvesting the berries. He watched her every move. He was madly in love with Hetty, and he longed to make her his wife, and not spoil her with his momentary passion. Arthur on the other hand was a steed pushing against a stable door. He was not all bad, but he was not all good like Adam Bede."

"The way you explain the relationships among the characters leads me to think you would be a great novel writer, Sara. You have a lot of inward passion. Why not bring some of that out?"

"I will have plenty to write about when we go home."

"Will you continue working at the newspaper?"

"Oh, yes, I can't let Mr. Cooper down. He depends on me."

"I see."

"No, you don't see. Mr. Cooper is like a father to me. His kids are grown, and have moved away. He told me that his son rarely visits him, and his daughter is in tight with her husband's family—so much so that they rarely see her. I suppose that happens when kids grow up."

"What if I were to tell you that I am all in favor of your spending time with Mr. Cooper?"

"Why?"

"It is good for you. He is good for you. He's gruff and demanding, but he cares."

"You intuit him well, Jacob. He is a kind old man wrapped in a hard shell. He may have been hurt many times in his life."

Jacob dropped his head. "Just listening to that story makes me sad."

"I love that about you, Jacob."

"Kiss me then. Kiss me like Hetty kissing Captain Donnithorne." He closed his eyes and leaned forward. My lips met his. It was like all of heaven rested on his mouth, and I was ascending to the open gate. Ecstasy!

"Let's read, Jacob."

"Now?"

"Yes, let's read *Adam Bede*."

"I'll get it." Jacob walked to the kitchen for my case. "Here it is."

"I love this book! It is her first novel. I want to write a novel like this. I wish to stir people's hearts." Jacob brought the wine closer as I read. "I love that we have mutual interests."

"Stephen King next! Equal time!" Jacob laughed as he tipped back his wine. "Will you return that book to Rosehill?"

"Perhaps. I tried that once. I was forced into the house because of a storm. I won't make that mistake again."

"Let's play-act Arthur and Hetty some more," Jacob laughed. The real thing is better than the book."

"I hear you!" The book slid out of my hands as I threw my arms around his neck. "Never have I felt this way with anyone else. But I'm glad you are not Arthur Donnithorne! You are his great-great grandson who is capable of putting love and respect before pleasure. I'm sure he is quite proud of you—if spirits can see."

"Listen," Jacob leaned away from me momentarily. I thought I heard laughter."

"Is the door locked?"

"Definitely! I will go look around outside though. Could be pranksters."

When Jacob returned, he shook his head. "It may have been a passing car full of joy-riders. It is a still night, and sound carries farther on still nights."

"Well, that flipped my mood. I think we should call it a night. I'm going to tuck in with my book."

"My mood hasn't flipped! Let's watch a movie."

"Some cheesy movie on a family channel?" I asked.

"Look, Sara, there's a British period film, *Pride and Prejudice*, on in five minutes."

"I've got all night! British period films rock. I think Mr. Darcy is terribly handsome, and the most eligible bachelor in any of Austen's books."

"Oh you do, do you?" Jacob did a Darcy imitation that made me beg for more. It was the kiss at the end— a soft, sweet kiss that speaks of deep affection.

"All I can say, Mr. Darcy, is that I am quite taken with you, with or without your cutaway coat."

"And Jane, dear, you are unlike any other girl I've known. Your head is full of notions that men have— notions of mystery and adventure. You are wild!"

"I'm wild about you! I know that much."

Jacob switched on the television. We lay back against the couch to immerse ourselves in the British period film that left every Austen fan swooning for more.

"Aren't the love scenes delicious?" I turned to see if Jacob was mesmerized too. He wasn't watching the movie; he was watching me.

"I think our love scenes are delicious! Jane and Darcy are just characters. We are the real thing. I'm so excited about our trip to Bath and Salisbury tomorrow that I can't concentrate on the movie. Speaking of which, we'd better get some sleep for our big day."

"Right! Goodnight. Until the morning then."

Jacob followed me to my bedroom door, kissed me and waited."

"Goodnight, Jacob!" The door closed against his face. I heard him groan as he padded down the hall to his room. Would I really sleep at all? Would he sleep? I bolted the door.

What Goes Around

Chapter 30

"I'm wearing my new red overcoat, Jacob. I have my shopping bag at the ready. It's another beautiful day. We should check out early. Jacob? Are you awake? I hate conversations through a closed door!"

Jacob walked up behind me from the kitchen. "Who are you talking to, Sara? Maybe your tall, dark-haired, and handsome Mr. Darcy? Or perhaps your tall, sandy-haired Captain Donnithorne?" I whirled around and cuffed him on the arm. He let out a big belly laugh, bending over with the amusement of it all.

"You think you're so funny! You startled me!"

"I'm sorry, but it was rather amusing watching you talk to the door like that. The cab is waiting, my bags are in. I'll help you with yours."

"You are so punctual, Jacob."

"I know. It's an old habit that works well for me."

"I have *Adam Bede* in my shopping bag." Jacob furrowed his brow. "I thought you loved reading as much as I."

"It has its place. Today is ours. *Adam Bede* gets packed."

"If you insist." It felt good to have Jacob making executive decisions. He helped me into the cab, then promptly shoved the novel deep into his travel bag.

"I'll lock up and leave a note for the Air B & B owners. Be right back." The cab trundled through the center of town. "Slower please, we want to check out the shops. We're going for breakfast first."

The cab driver acknowledged, "Sure, and you may want to try this one. He pointed to a quaint little shop with a bakery window full of decadent dessert pastries. "That's the best place in Stratford for pastries. Next is a little bakery on the other side of town across the street from Crabtree and Evelyn. They make a variety of fresh scones every day."

"Thank you, sir. We'll try both. Stop here and we'll walk down to the bakery after breakfast." Jacob handed him the fare. We began our day sitting at a bistro table inside the little shop sipping tea and eating buttery scones, double Devon cream and strawberry jam. Heaven!

"Everything here is quaint: streets, houses, shops." It is like walking inside a fairytale! The shop windows are like a box of Crayons. I didn't used to like so much color, or wear colorful clothes. I got stuck on neutrals. My clothes matched my mood, I guess. I love a punch of color now."

"Let's walk down to the bakery, Sara. We can get some baked goods for our train trip to Bath and Salisbury."

"Sounds delightful!" We started weaving our way west into town. A crosswalk helped us through a congested traffic area with a slow light. The bakery front was not impressive, but shoppers were pouring in and out like ants. We took a number and waited. "Two treacle tarts and two bakewell tarts please." The clerk passed us a box filled with premium pastries. It was tied at the top with string. So traditional.

"Let's cross over to Crabtree and Evelyn, Sara."

"Men don't like places like that. Are you suggesting it because you think I would like to look inside—not that I wouldn't want to look inside, but there are other things to do, and we have to catch a train."

"Follow me." Jacob took the packages and led the way to Crabtree and Evelyn. "They carry shortbreads and tea too, Sara."

"Will that be all, ma'am?" The clerk behind the counter rang up the order. Jacob came up from behind and told her to wait a moment.

"Would you like to try something?"

"How sweet of you. I don't wear much perfume. When I do, I prefer light, clean scents."

The clerk stepped from behind the counter and followed us to the back of the store. "This is our best hand cream. It has a fresh, clean fragrance, and you can wear it with your own favorite perfume. Gardener's Hand Therapy is a year 'round must have."

She handed me a sample. "Try this," she insisted.

"Lovely! Bright, fresh, innocent. And it makes my hands feel soft and silky. "I'll take it!"

The clerk bid us good day, and told us to stop back. We said we would, but there wasn't much chance of that.

"It's the perfect complement to your sweet smile. I should have thought of it sooner. Bloomingdale's tried to sell me this heady perfume that's all the rage now. It was so strong that a man might have worn it!"

"I'm certainly glad you did not buy that!"

"Let's take a quick tour of the town by bus—go out to the Anne Hathaway cottage. Who knows when we'll be back in Stratford."

"Let's. How romantic!" I was giddy. It was one of the few times in my entire life that I felt so high with anticipation. "The Anne Hathaway cottage today, Bath tomorrow, then Salisbury. What a treat!" We followed the signs down to the tourist information center. I sat on a bench with the packages while Jacob bought our tickets. Outside, tourists were walking to and fro. A red double decker bus was parked in the lot, and the driver was revving its engine.

"Is that our bus, Jacob?

"It is! Run!" He grabbed the packages, and we made a mad dash.

"Full tour?" The bus driver spouted like a parrot. He didn't even look up.

"Yes, sir." Jacob handed him our tickets.

"Mind your heads if you sit on the upper level. There are low-hanging branches during the rural portion of the tour." The bus driver closed the door as we raced for a seat. The guided tour began as we rocked through the historic streets of Stratford. Passing the Shakespeare homestead was a thrilling experience! Many of the houses on the tour were timber frame style—the typical cream stucco look with dark support beams. Some of the rooftops were thatched.

"We'll be leaving the town, and making our way out to Anne Hathaway's cottage and Arden Farm." The driver spoke with a monotone, but that didn't stop me from being enthusiastic about the ride.

"Let's go on the upper level, Sara."

"With all of these packages? And up that treacherous winding staircase?"

"We'll put the packages under the seat, and wait for him to stop at the next tourist site."

The upper level was exhilarating. My hair was in a tangle in less than sixty seconds, but I felt like a young girl on her first Ferris Wheel ride. Jacob seemed composed until a tree limb brushed the top of his head. We both laughed, ducking at the same time.

"There it is—up ahead! Anne Hathaway's cottage!" The multi-level thatched rooftop of soft gray was the most overwhelmingly beautiful site I'd ever seen. Next I noticed that the front yard was a rectangular English garden full of amazing specimens. "I wonder if George and George visited here? It seems like a *Mill on the Floss* kind of place. You know, Jacob, I almost feel as though I am British at heart—as though I belong here."

"In the nineteenth century, Victorian age, right? With George Eliot and George Lewes?"

"The history here takes one back many centuries, and I love them all."

"Sara, I am sure you would not have loved the plague in Shakespeare's time!"

"Touche´!"

We spent most of our time in the flower gardens and the large secluded orchard. The fresh air and birdsong captivated me. Jacob strolled along with his hands behind his back. He almost looked like one of the Royals. He said he had English roots.

"Unfortunately, the tour is over, Sara. We have to board the bus, and head back for the tourist center."

"I hate to leave this place, Jacob. It feels like home. It is rare for any place to feel like home to me. You don't speak of your parents, and I think I know why. My childhood was less than desirable. Perhaps you didn't have the best relationship with your parents either."

Ignoring my talk of family, Jacob addressed the thought of returning to Anne Hathaway's cottage someday. "We can tour another time, if you like, Sara. I love it too. It is pure and unspoiled. I'm sure most of that is due to preservation measures. But it sure tricks the mind into believing you are walking around in Anne Hathaway's time, sitting at her front fireplace on the deacon's bench listening to young Will Shakespeare read the first love poems he wrote for his blushing betrothed. Maybe Will stole a kiss when Anne's chaperone wasn't looking—like I'm going to steal one from you now!" The bus geared-up, and poor Jacob fell forward striking his head on the back of the seat. "I'm OK! I did that on purpose to make you feel sorry for me."

"Sure you did! You aren't really hurt are you?"

"Just this huge gash on my head." Jacob parted his hair to show me.

"Nothing!"

"I tried. I'm stealing a kiss anyway." The bus driver smiled in his rear view mirror. He had a personality after all!

"When we get back to the tourist center, we have to get a cab to the train station."

"And I need to check in with Mr. Cooper."

"So do I."

"What do you mean?"

"I mean, I have to check in with my boss too."

"Hello, Mr. Cooper? Can you hear me?"

"I haven't lost my hearing yet, Beck! Don't scream into the phone!"

"I'm in Stratford with Mr. Donnithorne. I took notes on a guided tour and several shops in the area. We are off to Bath and Salisbury as soon as we can get a train ticket."

"Did you check out my timeshare properties yet, Beck?

"No, I'm sorry, Mr. Cooper. But I think I have a bigger story here."

"Are you running the paper now, Beck?"

"Mr. Cooper!"

"That's my name. Listen, Beck, before you go down to Bath and lounge in the healing springs, drive out to the address I gave you for that new timeshare in the Midlands. Bring the other story back with you. I'll see if we can turn it into something. Ghosts of Rosehill Past, or maybe Griff Ghosts?"

"Very funny, Mr. Cooper." There was a click on the other end.

"That man exasperates me!"

"Whew, glad I'm not your boss. What has Coop-daddy done now?"

"Coop-daddy? Jacob, that is disrespectful."

"No, it's just humorous. I've been around men like that all my life, Sara. You have to find the humor in it. Don't let it bother you. The other option is to quit the job, and start writing novels."

"I don't have that luxury, Jacob. I have expenses. I live alone."

"Quitting a job is not something you decide to do overnight. Take your time and think it through. In the meantime, what does Mr. Cooper expect of you now?"

"He wants me to return to the Griff area and check on his timeshare property for him."

"Is that all?"

"What is the address of the timeshare property?"

"Let me dig into my briefcase and find the address. Mr. Cooper scribbled it on a piece of paper at the Second Street Diner. Here it is!"

"What don't you have in that briefcase, Sara?"

"The address is 715 D-something Way, Nuneaton."

"Is that the entire address?"

"Yes. His handwriting is terrible!"

"Let me see it. I'll do an area search in my real estate system. The only one I find is 715 Donnithorne Way. There's a coincidence!"

"Donnithorne Way? How can it be? Is there any connection to you?"

"It says little, just that this parcel belongs to a Mr. A.J. Donnithorne."

"You have living relatives in Warwickshire, Jacob?"

"Not necessarily in this case, Sara."

"You told me at Rosehill that you were a descendent of Arthur Donnithorne, Lord of Donnithorne Arms?"

"Yes, he was my great-great grandfather. The rascal. I'm told that his properties were sold by my cousin who squandered most of the money on women, drink, and gambling."

"The apple didn't fall far from the Donnithorne tree! Maybe this is what Marian was trying to warn me about."

"All Donnithornes are not created equal, Sara. I think this mystery needs solving. Get out your notebook and pen. We have work to do. Bath will have to wait. It is disappointing. I could use a hot spa right now."

"Yes, Bath—that magnificent city of limestone architecture and hot spas will have to wait." I heaved a sigh and reached for my notebook. Jacob and I were sniffing a story together. I took solace in that.

"What is that address again, Jacob? I'll correct it in my notes."

"It should read: 715 Donnithorne Way, Nuneaton. I'll get a cab. I guess we'll be back at Griff for the night. Let's drive out to the property on the way back to Griff."

"We have nothing better to do. And if, by chance, we solve the mystery today, we can continue our journey to Bath and Salisbury soon."

On the way to Nuneaton, we opened the bakery box, and ate the bakewell tarts for dinner. "So is life on the run," Jacob laughed. "We'll have a midnight snack at the Griff bar later."

"Are we getting close to Donnithorne Way, sir?"

"Another fifteen minutes or so, ma'am." I snuggled up next to Jacob. We held hands and watched the moonlight out of the cab window. Life was good— even in the back of a cab, snacking from a box, sniffing a story for Mr. Cooper aka Coop-daddy. The mature yew trees and rolling green hills of Warwickshire were mesmerizing. I was getting my fill of England's best.

"Here we are: 715 Donnithorne Way."

"Thank you, kind sir." Jacob handed the driver his fare and tip. There was a gate blocking the view of the building. We tested it. Locked. We turned back to the cab. "Can you wait?" Jacob asked. "It may take time for us to get inside the gate.

"Sure, no problem. Begging your pardon, sir, look now, there are lights coming down the lane." The cab driver was right; two long columns of light were coming at us down a lane that was hemmed in by tall trees. "That's a stretch limousine, sir. I've never been here before, but I'd guess that this is one of the rich Donnithorne's places."

"It's true," I gasped. "It's a Donnithorne property!"

"Well, I can't be sure, ma'am, but it looks that way. They own land all over these parts. I've seen others, but not this one." The driver was in awe, waiting for the long black limousine to come through the gates.

"Wait here," Jacob said. "I'll be right back." He ran to meet the driver as he passed through the gates.

"Stop. I need to ask you a question." The limousine kept driving, turning right toward town. Jacob ran inside the gate just in time before it fully closed. A few moments later, the gates opened again. "I found the emergency button inside the gate, Sara. Come on in."

"How exciting! Could you continue to wait, sir?"

"Sure, ma'am. I have no more fares this evening."

When I got inside the gates, Jacob pushed the button again to close them. We walked down the long line of linden trees. They had bloomed, and the heavenly scent of linden flowers perfumed the air. "The English call these lime trees. Do you find that odd?"

"There are many odd things about this place, Jacob."

"For an investigative journalist, you don't seem to be up for sleuthing, Sara."

"I'm a journalist who does mostly regional work. I've never sniffed a story in England—let alone aristocrats!"

"I don't think they are Royals; just wealthy." Security lights flashed in our faces as we neared the building. I heard barking dogs—large dogs. Thankfully they were behind a fence at the side of the property.

"Look at this, Sara. The sign over the door says Donnithorne, A.J., and the number 715."

"Oh my, it definitely is Donnithorne Arms!" When our eyes adjusted to the light, we could see four stories up.

"I'm going to get to the bottom of this." Jacob used the huge lion paw knocker to get attention. The door opened, and a butler stepped out.

"Welcome to Donnithorne Arms. Come in. May I take your overcoats?"

"Thank you, sir. Is the owner at home?"

"Home, sir, this is a hotel. Our rooms are timeshares. Are you a guest with us?"

"No, sir, but this lady, Miss Beck, has been asked to inspect the timeshare her boss plans to invest in here."

"The name, sir?"

"Cooper, Jacob Arthur."

"Feel free to look around, sir."

We walked up the long spiraling oak staircase to the second floor, then the third, then the fourth. A crystal chandelier hung three floors from the top, cascading down the center of the spiral staircase. Hundreds of lights refracting through the crystal cast geometric patterns on the scarlet stair treads.

"Which door should we try, Sara?"

"Seven has always been a lucky number for me. Let's count seven doors down to the right."

We entered the room. It was a suite sumptuously decorated. The finishing details were wanting, and it was apparent that the room was being decorated—or re-decorated, whatever the case. I got out my notebook and scratched down a few details.

"This place is like a castle, Jacob."

"It's a manor house, Sara. It may have been built in the eighteenth or nineteenth century."

"That old?"

"The older the house in England, the more it is worth to the British. They prize their history. Same with the Scots."

There was a sound in the hallway, and the suite door flew open. "Welcome to Donnithorne Arms!" A thin woman wearing a uniform with the Donnithorne crest on the pocket walked forward to hand us some sales literature. "I understand from the butler that you are interested in purchasing a timeshare?"

"Yes, Miss, my wife's boss is planning to buy into this property."

"How many rooms?"

"Just one suite, Miss."

"That's fine. That is what most do. Would you like to stay in one of the guest rooms for the night to see how you like it?"

"Oh, yes!" I answered before Jacob had a chance."

"Can we park your car for you? Bring your bags up? The kitchen is closed for the day, but I can bring you some cheese and wine."

"Perfect!" I said. "Red wine please."

"That won't be a problem, Miss. The name on the tab?"

"My name is Jacob, and this is my wife, Sara. We're the Coopers. Here is my credit card to reserve the suite. We already have our bags." She looked around suspiciously. "We've hung our clothes already. Thank you, Miss."

"My name is Miss Brook. I'll be right back with a tray and some of our vintage wine." We listened to make sure she went down the staircase.

"Did you hear that, Jacob?" Her name is Miss Brook! She's the nightmare hall stalker from Rosehill!"

"Relax, Brook is a common name. Besides, our door has a lock and chain. We will not allow anyone else in after she brings the tray. In the morning we will look around and see what we can discover for Coop-daddy."

"Oh no, we forgot about the cab driver! It's been thirty minutes at least!"

"Relax, Sara, I'll ring him up, and tell him to go on."

"There's only one bed, Jacob. And why did you lie to her and say we were Mr. and Mrs. Cooper? Your credit card says Donnithorne."

"It is a king size bed, Sara. I'll behave. If that doesn't work, then I'll sleep on the couch in the next room. Do not worry about the credit card. They rarely check the name."

The door swung open and in walked Miss Brook with a tray of aged cheeses, and red wine in a cooling urn.

"You'll find everything you need for the wine under the bar in the next room. Here is your card, sir. Sleep well."

"She knows, Jacob."

"Don't be silly. She said nothing."

"I'm telling you, she knows."

Jacob walked to the door, locked it, and put on the chain. "There, safe!"

"Rosehill left a mark on me, and I won't too soon be comfy with women in maids' uniforms, let alone one named Miss Brook! By the way, Jacob, can you sleep on the couch?"

"I said I would. I guess you don't trust me."

"It's not that, Jacob. I want our relationship to be a long and happy one. We have gotten off on the right foot. We don't want to spoil it now. Give us time."

"How could I say no to that?"

"Thank you, Jacob. Now I'll take my bath and slip on your extra white shirt for bed."

"I'm sure you look ravishing in a men's white shirt with…."

"Jacob!"

"OK, but one more thing, Miss Beck."

"Yes?"

"Will you marry me?"

"Oh, Jacob, are you serious—or are you trying to trick me into allowing you to sleep in the bed?"

"I love you, Sara. You don't have to answer now, but soon before I lose my mind traveling with you."

"I'm sure I won't sleep now, Jacob. No one has ever asked me to marry him before."

"I hope not!" Jacob laughed out loud. "We'll pick up an engagement ring at Bloomingdale's of London, and fly back to the States via Heathrow."

"I want something dainty—like Marian would wear. I can't wear a rock around the newspaper office."

"Not even in our castle?" Jacob laughed.

"Very funny!"

There was sudden pounding on the door next to our room. "Open up!" More pounding!

"Oh my god, I think it's the police, Jacob."

"You've got the wrong room. It's the next one down!" yelled a female voice in the outer hall.

"It's Miss Brook. I told you she was onto us! She's called the police!"

"Open up in there!" The knocking was at our door this time. Jacob walked calmly to the door, and opened it. The police stepped in. "ID please! Both of you!"

My hands were shaking as I took out my passport and driver's license. The policeman looked it over, and told me to sit down. He looked at Jacob's ID next, and his eyes almost bugged out of his head.

"Begging pardon, sir. I had no idea. The maid just told us that you were posing as the Coopers, and your credit card had another name on it. Have a good night, Mr. Donnithorne. You too, ma'am." The policemen backed out of the door, and closed it behind them.

"Did you check them out?" Miss Brook demanded of the police when they entered the hallway. We heard a thud, and ran to see what happened. Miss Brook had fainted, and the policemen were trying to revive her.

"Do you need any help?" Jacob asked as he leaned over Miss Brook's frail body. "She's on the ball, I can say that for her. She wouldn't let posers trick the establishment."

"Posers—now that's funny, Mr. Donnithorne. We will take care of Miss Brook. It's late, and the other Donnithornes will be coming back from a celebration dinner soon. Sorry to interrupt your evening with an official police visit. Enjoy your stay. "

We walked back to our suite. "Please open the wine, Jacob. We're going to celebrate our engagement."

"You aren't mad at me, Sara? I've been hiding the fact that I'm half owner of Donnithorne Arms, and several other real estate parcels here in England. In the morning, I will introduce you to my cousin, A.J. Donnithorne. He will try to toy with you. He is much like the one Marian warned you about."

"Do you mean all of this time you have lied to me? I've been bashing around England with a multi-millionaire, sneaking his clothes out of his room, borrowing his money all the way to England?"

"I tell very few who I really am in relation to the aristocratic Donnithornes. It helps to blend in. Old money knows how to handle those things."

"Old money? I don't believe this. I'm dreaming—just like at Rosehill! Why do you want me? I'm just a country girl from the Upper Midwest?"

"That is why I want you, Sara." Jacob walked into the room's bar and came back with something in his hand. He bowed down and asked me again to marry him. This is the ring I give you this night as a promise of our engagement. He slid an aluminum band from the wine bottle around my finger and pinched it to fit.

"I could do somersaults all night, I'm so happy! I think the house is happy too. Listen, do you hear it laughing, Jacob?"

"No somersaults. Let's do something safer, Sara."

"Like what? Read?"

• • •

"I love you, Jacob!"

"Sara? Sara, wake up. It's Miss Brook. Miss Matthews is here with me. You've had a terrible time for the last few days, my dear. Miss Matthews rode in the ambulance with you from Rosehill. We stopped in to see if you'd come 'round from the fall."

"Fall? What fall? Where am I?"

"You are in Worthing Hospital, Miss Beck. You hit your head when you fell at Rosehill. Do you remember returning the novel you borrowed? It was storming, and I asked you to come in and stay. It was a wicked storm, ma'am. Took out several of the houses in the area. Rosehill is closed. A mature tree fell on the old painted lady." Miss Matthews began to weep as she was explaining. "We thought we'd lost you."

"How long have I been in this place—this bed, Miss Matthews?"

"Three days. And a man named Mr. Cooper has been inquiring and stopping in to see you. He's terribly concerned."

"Do you mean I've been in this place for three days? Do I have a concussion, or what? How did I get here from England?"

"England, ma'am?" You've been here the whole time. Mr. Cooper mentioned that you were to go to England the same week of the storm, but I guess you weren't meant to go." Miss Matthews patted my brow with a cold cloth. I pushed her hand away.

"I have to get out of here and find Jacob."

"Jacob? Is that one of your co-workers?"

"No, he's my fiancée."

"Oh, Mr. Cooper told us you broke it off with...."

"What Miss Matthews means is that she didn't know you were engaged," said Miss Brook.

A nurse stepped into the room. "You've come around! We were sure you would with a little bed rest. You got cold-conked, Miss Beck. You've been in a coma. Take your time; sip some water. I'm going to check your vitals. Hungry? We'll get you a tray. Your friend, Sharon has been here every evening. And a Mr. Cooper is out in the waiting room now. He's been here every day too. I told him I'd check on you first before allowing visitors. Would you like to see him?"

"Of course!" I sat up in bed, feeling the pull of the intravenous tube. I retreated quickly.

"Take it slowly, ma'am. You'll have to find your legs again. You've been down awhile. Miss Brook and I will stop in again tomorrow—if that's OK?"

"If you like—thank you both for caring for me." They stepped out of the room, and Mr. Cooper stepped in. I was never so happy to see his big ornery face.

"Beck! The nurse told me you'd come around. It's about time. You'll be up and moving soon."

"Mr. Cooper, I'm sorry I didn't get your story. I flew to England though, and I stayed in George Eliot's homestead, the Griff. And then I went to Coventry, and Stratford. I met this man at the Rosehill B & B. He was so handsome. We flew to England together. He asked me to marry him when we stayed overnight at an English manor house. That was the last thing I remember. I'm engaged, Mr. Cooper! Why did I have to wake up; was it all a dream?" I began to weep.

Mr. Cooper leaned forward and patted my hand. "Sara, you didn't make it to England. But you will. There is no rush. In the meantime, I have someone I want you to meet. My son came to see me after so many years! It made my wife and me so happy. He's out in the waiting room. He met me here to go for lunch at the Second Street Diner. I'll go get him."

"Mr. Cooper, wait. Between us, I'm so happy for you and your family. Thanks for all you've done for me."

"Can I bring you something to eat? Melba toast and tea?" Mr. Cooper laughed.

"I'm famished! I could even eat some of your biscuits and gravy right now!"

"I'll be right back, Sara. You will love my son, I just know it." Mr. Cooper left the room and re-entered a few minutes later. "This is my son, Jacob, Sara. Jacob, this is Sara Beck, my best investigative journalist."

"Jacob! It's you!" The tall, sandy-haired man was taken aback.

"Sara, try to rest. I've explained to Jacob that you may suffer confusion and memory issues for a time. We will come to see you as we can. Jacob is here visiting from England for a month. When he goes back, I'm hoping you can go with him to check out the timeshares."

"Of course I'll go with Jacob. He is an expert in real estate matters."

"How do you know that, Sara?" Mr. Cooper looked at me strangely.

"I'm not sure, Mr. Cooper. Perhaps I heard you talking with your son at my bedside?"

"That's right, Dad, we talked about Sara going to England with me to check out the Donnithorne Arms."

"You're smiling, Sara. That's my girl! Good to have you back." Mr. Cooper leaned in and gave me an awkward hug.

"No worries about anything. Jacob and I will look after Cat. Sharon has been helpful too. She restocked your wine cupboard, and cleaned the cat's litter box." Mr. Cooper scratched his head to help himself remember. "Oh yes, and a package arrived at the newspaper office. It's from England, from an Albert at a Stratford Upon Avon address. Funny thing, the package has paint spatters all over it. Did you order a painting, Beck?"

Chills owned me. I *was* there! Albert was helping two people find each other. The painting is proof! It will bring us together again. My heart was racing as I looked at Jacob. He didn't know that I was his Hetty.

I'd been through trials, but none quite as severe as Hetty Sorrel's. I will rewrite the sad character Eliot painted so brilliantly in words. In my world, Hetty gets the guy, is respected in the community, and lives happily ever after. I have the passion of Hetty, but I never let it show. She was lace and sparkling reds; I am linen and nondescript neutrals. All of that is about to change. I lived through this head trauma for a reason. I was shown a future path should I choose it. I choose it!

"You're a million miles away, Beck. You must be sleepy. We'll see you tomorrow. Get some rest."

"Goodbye, Miss Beck. Charming to meet you. I know we'll have a mutually rewarding time exploring the timeshares in England."

"Don't be so stuffy, Jacob!" Mr. Cooper looked up at his son with a toothy grin. Jacob blushed.

"I look forward to seeing you again, Jacob," I said.

He left the room with his hands flung behind his back like a Royal, so shy and vulnerable—nothing like his father, Coop-daddy.

Just then, a young hospital volunteer stepped into my room with a lunch tray.

"I'm in love—with Jacob, with life, with grumpy Mr. Cooper, and yes, even with Miss Brook!" I shouted.

"What's that, Miss Beck?"

"Oh, nothing, I'm so happy to be alive! I've been given a second chance. I'm going to make the canvas of my life colorful—a Renoir—a masterpiece!"

"That's an optimistic attitude if I've ever heard one," said the volunteer. "Here's your tea and toast, Miss Beck. A man named Mr. Cooper ordered it for you."

"Oh no! Not more Melba toast." I lifted the plate cover. "It's British breakfast with a side of biscuits and gravy! Coop-daddy rides again!"

"There's a note for you too, Miss Beck."

I opened the coffee-stained napkin and read the scratchy handwriting. "Welcome to my world, Beck. You're gonna love it here! ~ Mr. Cooper"

∞

"It is never too late to be what

you might have been."

- Anon

Acknowledgements

I could not have written this novel without the input of **The George Eliot Fellowship**. My membership began in 2009, during which time, Chairman John Burton was extremely helpful with pictures, information on George Eliot, and even assistance with travel plans. In 2013, **John Burton and his wife, Lynda**, drove me around Warwickshire to the sites that were home to George Eliot through her young adulthood. Thanks to their consideration, I completed *Karma Road: Walking Through Time with George Eliot*, a nonfiction book paralleling the life of George Eliot to my own.

In 2015, I returned to the Warwickshire area to share *Karma Road* at the first **Writers in Warwickshire festival**. At that time, I met **Vivienne Wood**, vice chair of The George Eliot Fellowship and Shakespeare scholar and playwright. I am grateful for her friendship and support.

Crabtree and Evelyn – for their amazing products, and their quaint store in Stratford Upon Avon mentioned in this book.

Nuneaton Premier Inn & the Beefeater Restaurant at the Griff House – This fine Griff location, former home of British novelist George Eliot, is a lovely place to lodge and dine. Thank you for the opportunity to enjoy several days stay on two different occasions so that I could do research on George Eliot in 2013-2015.

Much gratitude to my daughter, **Vicki L. Lowery**, for being one of the proofreaders for *The House that Laughed*. Your critical eye and appreciation for a good story was of great help to me during the end stages of the book.

As always, my husband, **Norman R. Chaney**, has that English professor's eye for editing. I value his judgment when it comes to final touches.

I wish to thank the following people and recognize their wineries for the information I used in this book:

Palmeri Wines - The **Damskeys** are my good friends who own vineyards and produce wine in Northern California. **Kerry Damskey**, master winemaker, and international winemaking consultant, together with **Daisy Damskey**, his wife and partner, create small lot wines at Palmeri with the help of Kerry's son, **Drew Damskey**, whose particular skill is brand-building.

Dutcher Crossing Wines - Debra Mathy, winemaker at Dutcher Crossing, along with her dedicated staff, works to produce small lots of artisan wines in the Dry Creek Valley of Northern California. Debra's father, Charles Mathy, was her inspiration for the winemaking business. He passed away in 2006, and Debra carried on the business in honor of his memory.

Sula Vineyards - **Rajeev Samant** founded Sula Vineyards in 1998. In consultation with master winemaker, **Kerry Damskey**, Samant set up the first winery in the Nashik region of India northeast of Mumbai. Today Sula Vineyards it is the largest winemaking operation in India with a worldwide distribution, exporting to twenty six countries, and is listed with Marks & Spencers, a UK-based retail brand. Sula Vineyards was named in honor of Rajeev's mother, Sulabha.

Thank you to all of my **Facebook Friends** and other social media contacts who have supported and encouraged me throughout the writing of this novel.

Bibliography

Adams, Kathleen. *George Eliot: The Pitkin Guide*. Norwich: Jarrold Publishing, 2002.

Alexander, Catherine M.S. *Shakespeare: The Life, The Works, The Treasures*. London: Andre Deutsch, 2011.

Chaney, Freda M. *Karma Road: Walking Through Time with George Eliot*. USA: Freda M. Chaney/Createspace, 2015.

Eliot, George. *Adam Bede*. New York: John R. Alden Publisher, 1885.

Haight, G.S. *George Eliot, A Biography*. Oxford and New York: Oxford University Press, 1968: Reprint: Harmondsworth, Penguin Books, 1986.

Laski, Marghanita. *George Eliot*. London: Thames & Hudson, 1978.

McCutcheon, Marc. *The Writer's Guide to Everyday Life in the 1800s*. Cincinnati: Writer's Digest Books, 1993.

Scott, Sir Walter. *The Poems of Sir Walter Scott*. London: Oxford University Press, 1960.

Trewin, J.C. *The Pocket Companion to Shakespeare's Plays*. London: Octopus Publishing Group, 2005.

Uglow, Jenny. *George Eliot*. London: Virago Press, 1988.

Wordsworth, William. *The Poetical Works of Wordsworth*. London: Oxford University Press, 1961.

More Books
by
Freda Chaney

Karma Road:
Walking through Time with George Eliot

7 Days: Manifesting the Life You Want

House Blessings:
A Book about Cottage Living

Oh god, Papa!

Wisdom Talker

Bee Positive!
Illustrated by Vicki L. Lowery

Kate Won't Wait
Illustrated by Vicki L. Lowery

Available on Amazon

About the Author

Freda M. Chaney began writing when she was twelve. She attended Otterbein University, studying liberal arts, and earned a doctorate in divinity from AIHT. Freda has won awards for her poetry and short stories. Her periodical publications include *Angels on Earth* magazine and *Guideposts for Kids*. In addition, she has published in several literary magazines. Freda has eight published books to her credit. *The House that Laughed* is her first novel.

Chaney was born and raised in the state of Ohio, USA. She owns and manages a manor house B & B with her husband, Norman, who is a professor of English at Otterbein University. Together they search literary landscapes in books as well as in the real world.

Freda did much research in England to write her nonfiction book *Karma Road* about author George Eliot. By invitation, she read at the inaugural Writers in Warwickshire festival in 2015.

No trip to England would be complete without a visit to Stratford Upon Avon. The famous Anne Hathaway cottage, and the home of William Shakespeare stirred Freda's imagination while on tour with her husband in 2013. She returned with her daughter, Vicki, in 2015 to walk on foot around the town of Stratford, taking in details that were missed on an earlier bus tour. Freda's travel through rich British literary landscape culminated in the writing of *The House that Laughed*.

Further Information

Official website for
Karma Road: Walking Through Time with George Eliot
by Freda M. Chaney

www.karmaroadwalkingthroughtime.com

George Eliot video tour
with John Burton and Freda Chaney

http://youtu.be/2s8rZ6SdI8k

Official website for The Chaney Manor B & B
owned by Norman and Freda Chaney

www.thechaneymanorbb.com

Seek and Find

There is an artist whose name is
mentioned inside this book.
His name is also hidden
in the back cover
artwork.

See if you can find it.

Made in the USA
Monee, IL
19 August 2022